SeaHorses

Gathering Storm

Bor tfordshire, Eng. May 1952, Louise Cooper descri her a al scatter-brained Gemini'. She spent m of r sc ol years writing stories when she should have been concentrating on lessons, and her first fantasy novel, *The Book of Paradox*, was published in 1973, when she was just twenty years old. Since then she has published more than sixty books for adults and children.

Louise now lives in Cornwall with her husband, Cas Sandall. When she isn't writing, she enjoys singing (and playing various instruments), cooking, gardening, 'messing about on the beach' and – just to make sure she keeps busy – is also treasurer of her local Royal National Lifeboat Institution branch.

Visit Louise at her own web site at
www.louisecooper.com

In the same series

Sea Horses

Gathering Storm

Louise Cooper

PUFFIN

PUFFIN BOOKS

Published by the Penguin Group
Penguin Books Ltd, 80 Strand, London WC2R 0RL, England
Penguin Group (USA), Inc., 375 Hudson Street, New York, New York 10014, USA
Penguin Books Australia Ltd, 250 Camberwell Road, Camberwell, Victoria 3124, Australia
Penguin Books Canada Ltd, 10 Alcorn Avenue, Toronto, Ontario, Canada M4V 3B2
Penguin Books India (P) Ltd, 11 Community Centre, Panchsheel Park, New Delhi – 110 017, India
Penguin Group (NZ), cnr Airborne and Rosedale Roads, Albany, Auckland 1310, New Zealand
Penguin Books (South Africa) (Pty) Ltd, 24 Sturdee Avenue, Rosebank 2196, South Africa

Penguin Books Ltd, Registered Offices: 80 Strand, London WC2R 0RL, England

www.penguin.com

First published 2004
3

Copyright © Louise Cooper, 2004
All rights reserved

The moral right of the author has been asserted

Set in Adobe Sabon
Typeset by Rowland Phototypesetting Ltd, Bury St Edmunds, Suffolk
Made and printed in England by Clays Ltd, St Ives plc

British Library Cataloguing in Publication Data
A CIP catalogue record for this book is available from the British Library

ISBN 0–141–31441–9

*With grateful thanks to Pol Hodge,
who turned Tamzin's summoning spell
from English to Cornish – and a special
hello to Chloe Melwynn!*

'There is a legend,' said Nan quietly, 'about two spirits that once haunted this coast. They were known as the Blue Horse and the Grey Horse, and they came from the sea. The Blue Horse brought fair weather, and protected the sailors and fishermen. But the Grey Horse was cruel. He brought storms and treacherous tides, and took delight in wrecking ships and drowning the men on board.

'At last, the two spirits fought a terrible battle. There were gales and huge, raging tides, and the people of the coast were terrified that the Grey Horse would win and destroy them all. But one fisherman's family was not afraid. They joined forces with the Blue Horse and between them they overcame the Grey Horse and defeated him.

'When the battle was over and the people

were safe, an old, wise woman of the fisherman's family carved a little stone statue. The evil power of the Grey Horse was imprisoned in the statue, and the family pledged to keep it for always.' Nan turned a piercing gaze on Tamzin. 'They were our ancestors. And the legend says that if the statue should ever be broken, the dark spirit will be released again.'

Silence fell. Then, in a quavering voice, Tamzin whispered, 'And I broke it . . .'

chapter one

When Tamzin Weston woke up in the middle of the night, she was instantly aware of two strange things. First, her room seemed to be shaking very slightly; the mattress underneath her quivering, ornaments rattling on the shelves and dressing table. And second, downstairs she could hear her nan's fluffy black cat, Baggins, howling.

'Baggins?' Tamzin sat upright, feeling for the switch of her bedside lamp.

The light came on and she scrambled out of bed. But as she tried to stand up the room seemed to lurch, like the deck of a ship in a rough sea. Tamzin staggered and almost fell over. She could hear a low rumbling sound, though it was very faint. *Thunder?* she thought. But thunder didn't make everything shake like a jelly.

Then along the passage a door banged, and a familiar voice called out, 'Tamzin, are you all right?'

Tamzin stumbled to the door and opened it, to see Nan, in her dressing gown, on the landing. 'Nan!' she cried. 'What's happening?'

'I'm not sure.' Nan's black hair was loose and curling around her shoulders. 'But whatever it is, it's terrifying poor Baggins. I'd better go and rescue him.'

She started down the stairs. The shaking seemed to have stopped now, but Tamzin was afraid that at any moment it might start again and send Nan tumbling head over heels to the bottom. She waited, holding her breath, until she heard the click of the downstairs door latch. A second later Baggins came streaking up the stairs, ears flattened on his head and his tail fluffed out like a bottlebrush. He shot into Tamzin's room and dived under the bed.

'Poor old thing!' Nan came in and crouched down to peer under the bed. 'Come on, Baggins. Come on, puss; it's all right. There's nothing to be scared of.'

The only answer was a kind of 'wowrrr' noise and Baggins didn't emerge. Nan straightened. 'Well, whatever it was, it seems to have stopped now.'

She spoke too soon. As she said the word 'now', a new and more powerful vibration juddered through the house. Tamzin squealed in fright, Nan lost her balance and reeled against the bed. The ornaments rattled crazily, almost dancing on their shelves. And suddenly one of the pictures on the wall broke loose and fell to the floor with a terrific crash.

Then, shockingly, everything was still and silent.

Wide-eyed, Tamzin and Nan stared at each

* ★ ★

other. Nan was breathing deeply, and Tamzin's heart pounded under her ribs like a hammer. Neither of them said a word. Then Tamzin turned and looked at the fallen picture, which lay face up on the floor.

It was one of Nan's own paintings, and it showed a white horse galloping out of a moonlit blue-and-silver sea. Under the moon, the horse's coat was tinged blue. The picture was very special to Tamzin. And it was the only one that had fallen.

'Oh, Nan . . .' Tamzin's voice was a thin, frightened whisper. 'Why *that* one, and none of the others?' She hurried to lift the painting up. 'The frame's broken!'

Nan came to look. 'The picture itself isn't damaged.' She studied Tamzin's face. 'Love, I know what you're thinking. But whenever something happens, it doesn't always mean the Grey Horse is behind it.' She smiled kindly. 'There *is* such a thing as coincidence, you know.'

* * *

Tamzin nodded and tried to smile back.

'Look,' Nan added, pointing. 'Here's Baggins coming out. Everything must be all right now: animals always know.'

Baggins emerged from under the bed and gazed up at them. His tail was back to normal and he looked a little bit sheepish.

'What was it, Nan?' Tamzin asked.

'I don't know for certain,' said Nan, 'but I think it might have been an earth tremor. It's like a mini-earthquake; we do get them here in Britain, more often than most people realize. Mostly, though, they're so small that no one notices.' She put her arm round Tamzin's shoulders and gave her a reassuring squeeze. 'Anyway, it's over. Look at Baggins; he's curling up on your bed. He'll go back to sleep now – and so should we.'

'Can he stay in my room tonight?' Tamzin asked.

Strictly speaking, cats on beds were against the rules, but Nan smiled. 'Of course he can, just this once. Will you be all right now?'

Tamzin hesitated, looking at the picture. 'I *think* so,' she said at last.

Nan understood. 'I'll mend the frame first thing in the morning,' she promised. 'Go on; back to bed. Leave your light on, if you want to.'

She kissed Tamzin and went out, and Tamzin climbed back under her duvet. Baggins closed his eyes, made a happy noise and stretched his front paws out to claim more than his fair share of the bed, but she didn't mind. She stroked him and he started to purr. It was comforting. It made her feel a lot better. She didn't need the light on.

She switched the lamp off, and settled down to go to sleep.

At breakfast time the local radio news was bubbling with the story of the strange shaking in the night. Nan had been right; it was an earth tremor, centred, the newsreader said, some way out to sea off the Isles of Scilly. Most of Cornwall had felt it, but it had been strongest along the north coast, where Nan lived.

'I wonder if it's done any damage,' Nan said, as they ate toast.

'Damage?' Tamzin looked up quickly.

'Along the beaches. We sometimes get rockfalls in the big winter storms, that bring down pieces of the cliffs.' She looked out of the kitchen window. 'It's a nice day, and the tide will be low by lunchtime. I might walk to our beach and see if anything's happened.' Then a smile spread across her face. 'An earth tremor, eh? That'll be something to tell your mum and dad when they phone tonight, won't it!'

Tamzin's parents were in Canada, where Dad was working for a year. His work involved travelling a great deal, so Tamzin had been sent to live with Nan while they were away. It was hard to believe that five months had already passed since she came here. She had expected the time to drag horribly. But though she missed her parents, life in Cornwall had turned out to be anything but boring. She and Nan had become close friends; and Tamzin had made other friends, too – in particular a boy a year or so older than her, whose name was Joel Richards. Joel lived a short way up the valley from Nan's house, and his parents owned and ran a riding stable. Horses were Tamzin's great passion, but in her city home she had never had the chance to learn to ride. Now, that had all changed. At weekends and in the school holidays she helped at the stables in exchange for riding lessons, and Joel said now that she was almost as good as he was. That wasn't true, of course, for Joel had started riding almost as soon as he could walk. But her dearest dream had come true.

Yet with the dream had also come a nightmare . . .

* * *

The painting with the broken frame was in Nan's studio now, waiting to be mended, and the thought of it sent an unpleasant shiver down Tamzin's spine. *Broken*. It brought back the memory of the little stone statue of a grey horse, centuries old, that had been passed down through the family and kept safe . . . until she had defied Nan's warning and taken it from its shelf when no one was about. Even after five months Tamzin had a clear and awful memory of how the statue had seemed to writhe and twist in her hands, before it fell from her grasp and shattered in pieces on the floor.

Tamzin's dismay at breaking the statue had turned to horror when Nan finally told her why she should never have touched it. There was a legend, Nan said, of two spirits: the Blue Horse, bringer of calm seas and fair weather, and the Grey Horse, who hated humankind and blighted the land with storms and gales. When the Grey Horse threatened to wreak disaster on the coast and the people who lived here, Nan's own ancestors had called on the spirit of the Blue Horse to save them. The two powers battled; with the help of his human friends the Blue Horse was victorious, and the Grey Horse's spirit was imprisoned in a stone statue, and entrusted to the family to keep safe for always. Now, the statue was broken, and the evil power of the Grey Horse had been set free again. It wanted revenge – revenge on the family who had trapped it for so long. And Tamzin was its target.

Tamzin had desperately wanted to believe that the legend could not be true. But twice now she had faced the Grey Horse, and it had nearly succeeded in killing her. It had not given up. It would *never* give up. Unless it could be captured and imprisoned once more, she would be in danger.

Her hand went to a silver chain bracelet around her wrist, and she fingered a strangely shaped pendant that hung from it. The pendant was formed from two pieces of glass, of different shades of blue. Tamzin had found one piece after her first terrifying encounter with the Grey Horse, the other after her second . . . and some mysterious magic had caused them to fuse together, to form a delicate, curving shape. The pendant was her talisman, for she was sure it was a gift from the Blue Horse; a sign that the benevolent spirit was trying to reach out and help her. But the link was so fragile. The Grey Horse's power was growing, and still she had not found a way to make contact with the Blue Horse.

And now there had been an earth tremor . . .

Nan started to clear the breakfast dishes, and the clatter brought Tamzin down to earth. With a great effort she pushed her thoughts away. Nan had been right last night; there *was* such a thing as coincidence. She had to hold on to that, believe in it, and think about other things. Such as the fact that the weather was lovely and the Easter holidays were just beginning, which meant three whole weeks of riding stretching ahead of her like a happy dream.

Nan saw her change of mood and smiled. 'I can see you're itching to get along to the stables,' she said, 'and on a day like this I don't blame you. I'll let you off the washing up – go on, go and get ready.'

'Brilliant!' Tamzin jumped to her feet and gave Nan a hug. 'Thanks, Nan! I'll see you later!'

chapter two

Though it was still only March, the
weather was warm enough for a lot of
the riding stable horses to have been turned
out in the field. Barney, the Richardses' woolly
dog, barked joyfully when he saw Tamzin
approaching, and the horses too came
crowding to the field gate to greet her, hoping
for titbits. Tamzin took chunks of apple and
carrot from her bulging jacket pockets and
shared them around. She knew each horse by
name now, and greeted them: 'Hello, Sally-
Ann, Dandy, Rosie – oh, Pippin, you
greedyguts; stop pushing in!' But all the while

she was looking for one pony in particular. Moonlight was pure white with just a hint of dapple grey on his quarters and legs. He was Tamzin's favourite – and far more than that, he was a very special friend. For twice now, when the Grey Horse had threatened her life, Moonlight had come to her rescue . . .

But Moonlight wasn't in the field this morning. At last Tamzin left the gate and walked to the stable yard with Barney trotting at her heels.

'Hi!' A dark head appeared at one of the loose-box doors, and Joel waved to her. 'I'm mucking out.' He pulled a face. 'I could do with some help!'

'OK.' Tamzin grinned. Mucking out was messy and smelly, as its name suggested, but she didn't mind. 'Where's Moonlight?' she asked.

'In his box. He's booked for a customer this morning, so you'll have to ride another pony when we go out.'

* * *

'Oh. Well, I'll go and say hello to him, then I'll give you a hand.'

Moonlight must have heard her voice, for the next moment he was whickering at the door of his box, tossing his head up and down and eager to nuzzle Tamzin's face and hands as she hurried to him. She gave him two apples she had saved for him and he crunched them happily then blew on her fingers for more.

'It's all gone.' She rubbed him between the ears, where his forelock flopped over his eyes. 'We can't go out together this morning, Moonlight. I'm sorry. But maybe tomorrow.'

'Come on, Tam!' Joel called. 'Or I'll be finished before you've even started!'

She gave Moonlight a final pat and went to join him.

As they mucked out, Tamzin and Joel talked about the earth tremor. The Richardses had all felt it, too; Barney had gone crazy, Joel said, and the horses had been so frightened that the family had had to go out to the stables in the dark to calm them. Luckily, though, no damage had been done, though it had been frightening while it lasted.

'Nan says tremors happen quite often,' Tamzin told him.

'Mmm.' Joel's face clouded. 'I don't know. *I've* never felt one before. And I can't help wondering . . .'

'What?' she prompted when he didn't finish.

'Ohh . . . Nothing.' His expression cleared. 'Come on. Let's forget about it, and get on with the work. The sooner we finish, the sooner we can go riding!'

An hour later, they left the stables and rode down the valley path to the beach. Joel was on piebald Dandy, while Tamzin rode a pretty little mare called Lark, who was dark brown with a white star and four white socks. The sun was bright and warm, and the sea, between the 'V' of the cliffs to either side, was a brilliant sapphire blue.

* * *

They guided the ponies carefully down
the boulder-strewn slope that led from the car
park on to firm golden sand. The tide was
going out, and it was possible to get round
the headland.

'If we go round to the left, we can have a
gallop,' Joel said.

'Lovely!' Tamzin pressed her heels to Lark's
sides and the ponies broke into a trot. As they
rounded the jutting headland, the huge
expanse of the beach stretched out before
them. Wet sand shone at the sea's edge, and
the crests of the big breakers glittered in the
sunlight. At first they thought the beach was
deserted, but then Joel pointed to a lone figure
walking near the rocks at the foot of the cliffs.

'Isn't that your nan?' he asked.

Tamzin shaded her eyes. 'Oh, yes – she
said she was going to come down, to see
if there have been any rockfalls. Let's go and
meet her.'

The ponies were eager to gallop, but Joel

* * *

and Tamzin restrained them to a canter as they rode towards Nan. Nan saw them and waved, then pointed at the cliffs.

'Wow!' Joel said, as he saw what she was indicating. 'There's been a rockfall, all right! Look at that!'

There were caves in the cliffs, and the next one along was the largest of all. It had an entrance like a gaping mouth. Or rather, it used to have. Now, the mouth was completely blocked by a pile of enormous, jagged-edged boulders, piled one on top of another and spreading on to the sand. Above the cave was a great new V-shaped scar that ran down from the clifftop, showing where the chunks of rock had broken away.

Tamzin stared in astonishment. 'That's *incredible*!' she said.

Joel nodded. 'Just shows how unstable these cliffs can be. Come on, let's go and see your nan.'

As they approached, they saw someone

else standing at the foot of one of the fallen boulders. He was talking to Nan, and as the ponies arrived Nan turned to greet them.

'Hello!' she said. 'Spectacular, isn't it? This is Mr Brewer – he's here on holiday. This is my granddaughter, Tamzin, and her friend Joel.'

'Hello.' The man, who was about Nan's age, smiled at the two riders. 'Pleased to meet you.' He had a pleasant, friendly face, with thinning fair hair and a bushy beard. He didn't look like a beach holidaymaker; more like a hiker, with a belted jacket, heavy boots and trousers tucked into his thick socks. Near him on the sand was a canvas shoulder bag with a flashlight strapped to it.

Mr Brewer saw Joel looking curiously at the bag, and grinned. 'Mrs Weston isn't strictly right about the holiday bit. I'm here to do some research. Or I was, until this happened.' He waved a hand towards the rockfall. 'I've been told that there are some old tunnels and air shafts that link up with this cave. People say they were dug by miners, but I've got a theory that they're a lot more ancient than anyone realizes.'

'Are you an archaeologist?' Tamzin asked.

'Yes. My special interest is ancient Cornwall, and this area in particular. My ancestors came from here, way back, you see.'

'Did they?' Joel asked. His voice sounded a little sharp, Tamzin thought. 'Whereabouts?'

'Well, I'm not *exactly* sure where – or even when, for that matter. But it was certainly within a few miles. And a very long time ago.' He smiled again. 'Too long ago for me to call myself Cornish, I'm afraid!'

Nan and Tamzin both laughed, but Joel did not. His face was very serious, and he seemed to be thinking hard. Before he could say anything, though, Mr Brewer continued.

'I gather your family has been here a long

time, too, Tamzin. Your nan knows a lot about local history.'

'Oh, yes, she does,' Tamzin agreed. From the corner of her eye she saw Joel giving her a strange look, but she ignored it. Mr Brewer turned to Nan again.

'I don't know if you'd be willing, Mrs Weston, but I'd love the chance to talk to you about that. Your knowledge might help me to a few short cuts with my research.'

'I'd be delighted,' said Nan. 'I tell you what: why don't you come to tea this afternoon, if you're not busy?' She nodded towards the cave. 'You're not going to make much progress here, after all.'

He beamed. 'I'd like that very much!'

'Then it's settled. Chapel Cottage isn't too difficult to find; it's just –'

'Tam, shall we ride on?' said Joel quietly, as Nan started to give directions.

Tamzin blinked, surprised. 'What? All right, then. If you're in a hurry.' She glanced at Nan

* * *

for permission, Nan smiled and nodded, and
Mr Brewer said, 'See you later, I hope,
Tamzin.'

'Yes,' said Tamzin. 'I'll look forward to it.'

Joel was waiting, and as Tamzin gathered
up her reins ready to go, he suddenly dug his
heels into Dandy's flanks. Dandy took off at
a gallop, sand scattering from his hooves.

'Hey!' Tamzin shouted. 'What about our
race? You said you'd give me a head start!'

Joel called back but she couldn't hear what
he said. Dandy was already almost at the sea's
edge and Lark pranced, wanting to gallop too.
What on earth was the matter with Joel?
Tamzin sighed, then gave Lark her head and
they set off in pursuit with the wind flying in
their faces.

She only caught up with Joel when he halted
Dandy near the far end of the beach.

'Joel,' she said, 'what's the matter?'

For a few moments Joel didn't reply, but

stared out to sea. Then at last he said, 'It's that man.'

'Who? Mr Brewer?'

'Yes. I don't trust him.'

'You don't even *know* him!'

'Exactly,' said Joel. 'And I think it's a bit weird that he should just happen to turn up when he did.'

The ponies were standing in the shallow water at the sea's edge. Lark put her head down and snorted at the small wavelets.

'Look,' Joel went on, very quickly as though he wanted to get the words out before his nerve failed, 'what if the earth tremor wasn't a coincidence? Then the morning afterwards, a stranger suddenly comes along and gets involved with us. Well, that's happened once before, hasn't it? At Christmas. And you know as well as I do what it led to!'

'You mean . . . Marga?'

'Yes.' Joel took a deep breath. 'What I'm saying is, how do we know that this Mr

* * *

Brewer isn't something to do with the Grey Horse as well? This could be a trap, Tam. Just like last time!'

Tamzin sighed. Joel had not wanted to believe in the Grey Horse at first. But what had happened at Christmas had changed his mind. He had allowed himself to be fooled, and his mistake had almost ended in disaster. Since then he had felt guilty, and now he was suspicious of everyone and everything. The smallest incident, to him, was a new sign of the Grey Horse's power, and he saw – or imagined – threats around every corner.

'Joel,' she said, 'this is crazy! We can't go around suspecting everyone we meet of working for the Grey Horse. Mr Brewer seems perfectly OK to me.'

'Then why is he so interested in that particular cave? We both know what happened there last year!'

Tamzin shuddered as she recalled that night, when she had had her first direct encounter

24

* * *

with the Grey Horse. But she pushed the
memory away and said, 'There's such a thing
as coincidence. That's what Nan said last
night. She's no fool. If there was anything
fishy about Mr Brewer, she would have
sensed it. And she certainly wouldn't have
invited him to tea!'

'She might be wrong, though. Mightn't she?'

'OK, she *might*. But I don't think she is.
She never met Marga, remember. If she had,
things might not have gone wrong the way
they did. I trust her, Joel. Can't you do the
same?'

Joel shrugged. 'I want to. But . . .'

'*Please*. We can't let this get to us, or we'll
both go nuts with worrying all the time.'

He paused. Then at last he let out a long
breath. 'All right,' he said. 'I'll try. But do me
a favour, will you? Just be careful.'

'Of course I will,' said Tamzin.

chapter three

M r Brewer's teatime visit was a great success. He and Nan were soon on first-name terms, and he insisted that Tamzin, too, should call him Alec. He was very interested to learn all that Nan could tell him about local history, and he had quite a few pieces of information of his own to add.

Then, as they were finishing the last of Nan's home-made ginger cake, he said something that gave Tamzin a jolt.

She had been joining in the talk, but at that moment she was sneaking titbits under the table to Baggins, who loved cake of any kind.

So she was not really paying attention when Alec said, 'And of course there's the old tale about a disaster that happened round here centuries ago. Did you know about that?'

'A disaster?' Nan frowned. 'No, I've never heard of it.'

'Ah!' said Alec. 'Not many people have, I gather. But I found it in an old book; written in the nineteenth century, I think. The book was very vague, because even then the tale was almost forgotten; it was something about a flood, or a tidal wave, that threatened to destroy the coastal villages.'

Tamzin's head came up sharply and she stared at Alec.

'The writer didn't say whether it did destroy them,' Alec went on. 'He obviously didn't know. But according to him, the local people certainly used to *believe* that something terrible had happened.'

Tamzin was wide-eyed. *A flood, or a tidal wave, centuries ago . . .* Could it be connected with the legend of the battle between the Blue and Grey Horses?

She looked at Nan, and found that Nan was already looking at her. Tamzin desperately wanted to ask Alec how much more he knew, but she couldn't find the words to begin. Then Nan gave a tiny little shake of her head. It wasn't enough for Alec to notice, but it warned Tamzin to say nothing.

'If the disaster story is true,' Alec went on, 'then it seems that it happened along this stretch of coast. The book I saw mentioned your beach, and a passage through the cliffs that was an escape route of some kind; though again it was all very vague. So when I heard about the tunnels in that cave, I hoped I might find some clues to what actually happened.' He smiled ruefully. 'Now, though, it doesn't look as if I'll get the chance.'

'I'm not so sure about that,' said Nan thoughtfully. 'If you can't get to the cave from the bottom, how about trying from the top?'

* * *

'The top?' Alec's face brightened. 'Do you think it's possible?'

'I don't know. But there are all manner of clefts and gullies up on the cliffs. There *might* be a way through, provided you were careful.'

Alec grinned. 'I've been in enough tricky situations to be very careful indeed! Really, Isobel: you think it would be worth a try?'

'Yes,' said Nan. 'I do.' She caught Tamzin's eye again. 'I definitely do.'

Alec left an hour later. Nan had told him how to explore the clifftop by the safest paths, and he planned to go and investigate the following morning.

When he had gone, Tamzin was eager to talk to Nan about the disaster tale he had told them.

'I wanted to ask him if he's ever heard about the Grey Horse,' she said. '*Do* you think there could be a connection, Nan?'

'If the disaster really happened, then I think

29

there could,' said Nan gravely. 'But I also think we should be careful.'

'You mean, you don't trust Alec?' Cold, invisible spiders ran down Tamzin's back as she remembered what Joel had said. But Nan shook her head.

'It isn't that, love. I like Alec, and I'm as sure as I can be that there's nothing suspicious about him. But he isn't the kind of person who would believe in anything supernatural. He wouldn't take the Grey Horse seriously; he'd think it was just an old story that someone made up.'

Tamzin was crestfallen. 'So he'd laugh?' she said.

'Well . . . maybe not. But he wouldn't believe. So I think it's best if we don't tell him too much about it, at least not for the time being.' Nan paused. 'Mind you, I wouldn't mind seeing what he *does* uncover. You never know: it might prove very useful . . .'

*

* * *

Tamzin was at the stables early the next day. She had thought hard about Nan's advice, and she had decided that there could be no harm in her riding up the cliff path this morning, to see whether Alec had managed to find a way to get into the cave.

The only problem was Joel. Tamzin wanted to tell him about her plan and ask him to go with her; but she knew how he would react. All his suspicions would come to the surface again. He would probably refuse to go, and if she said she was going alone he would probably try to stop her. She didn't want to quarrel with him. But how could she persuade him to do what she asked?

She was still dithering about what to do when she reached the stables. However, the problem was solved for her – because Joel was not there.

'His mother's taken some customers out on a half-day trek,' said Mr Richards, who was in the stable yard. 'There are quite a lot of them,

31

* * *

so Joel's gone along to help. They won't be back until after lunch.' He smiled at her. 'Tell you what, there isn't much work to do this morning. Why don't you go for a ride on your own? You can take Moonlight; he isn't booked today.'

It was the ideal answer to Tamzin's dilemma. If Joel wasn't here, he couldn't argue about going to the clifftop. She would tell him later, and if he wasn't happy about it – well, by then it wouldn't matter, because she would have found out what she wanted to know. And she would be perfectly safe, she thought. Yesterday on the beach, she had been riding Lark. Today, though, she would be on Moonlight. And if Alec Brewer couldn't be trusted, Moonlight would know.

She groomed Moonlight, then saddled him and rode out of the yard. She knew her way around the paths pretty well by now, and took the wider, inland track that would bring her out at the top of the high cliffs. The day was

* * *

sunny again, and as they reached the top the whole sky opened out like a brilliant, upside-down blue bowl. The sea was blue, too, moving like silk as the swell rolled in. It was a good omen, Tamzin thought.

She turned Moonlight along another path towards the headland above the cave. The cliff sloped quite gently towards it, and the path led to a natural, shallow dip directly over the cave. As she approached, Tamzin could see that the grass and heather were scoured away where the rock had fallen; she halted Moonlight at the edge of the dip and looked down.

Alec was there, at the bottom of the dip where the path ended. He was digging around with a trowel, and Tamzin saw that there was a narrow, gaping fissure in the rock near where he stood.

He looked up, saw her and waved. 'Hello!'

'Hello!' Tamzin called back. 'Have you found anything interesting?'

'I certainly have! See this hole? I'm pretty sure that it goes right through to a tunnel. I just need to clear a bit more of this loose earth away, so I can get a proper look.'

'Could I come down and see?' Tamzin asked.

'Certainly!'

Tamzin tapped Moonlight's flanks gently with her heels and the pony started down the path again. But they were no more than halfway to Alec when Moonlight suddenly stopped.

'Come on, Moonlight!' Tamzin urged. 'Come on. What's the matter?'

She tried to make him move again, but Moonlight flatly refused. He stamped and pawed, backing away and almost sitting down on his haunches. Tamzin tried to get him under control, but he fought her, shaking his head, snorting and dancing sideways. He was making such a fuss that to stay on his back could be dangerous, so Tamzin quickly slid

from the saddle and went to his head, trying
to calm him down.

'Are you having trouble?' Alec called.

'He's never like this normally!' Tamzin was
breathless. 'Stop it, Moonlight! Quiet, now!'

'Hang on,' said Alec. 'I'll come and help.'

He started up the path. But as he reached
them, Moonlight became even more agitated.
He shied away from Alec, almost rearing,
dragging Tamzin with him as he backed
further up the path.

'Here, let me,' said Alec. He reached out to
grasp Moonlight's bridle – and, so fast that
Tamzin hardly saw it happen, Moonlight's
head snaked out. He clamped his teeth on
Alec's arm; Alec yelped with surprise and tried
to pull free. But Moonlight would not let go.

'*Moonlight!*' Tamzin cried. Moonlight took
no notice. He yanked at Alec, at the same
moment scrabbling backwards and towing
Tamzin on the end of the reins. As Alec lost
his balance and stumbled, there was an

ominous grumbling sound beneath them. The ground underfoot seemed to shiver – then the grumbling swelled to a groan, and a whole section of the path where Alec had been standing started to slither away. Alec yelled '*Look out!*' and suddenly the three of them were stumbling and scrambling to get clear as a mini-avalanche of rocks and stones and earth went sliding and tumbling down into the dip. They struck the fissure at the bottom; there was a *crack*, and the fissure widened to a gaping mouth, into which all the rolling debris vanished with an echoing roar.

Tamzin had tripped and fallen as she reached the top of the path, and now she sat staring dazedly at the huge, dark hole where moments before there had been solid ground. A metre away, Alec was getting to his feet. His face was pale and he looked shocked. When he spoke, his voice was shaking.

'The tremor must have loosened more rock

than I realized . . .' He turned and looked at Moonlight, and swallowed. 'Your pony saved our lives.'

Moonlight was standing rigid, head high, nostrils flared, and Tamzin realized the truth. The pony had *known* that the landslide was about to happen, and when he grabbed Alec's arm, it had not been an attack but an effort to pull him clear in time. Then following that thought came another that frightened her. Yes; Moonlight had saved their lives. But where had the threat come from? Could it be that the Grey Horse knew exactly where they were at that moment, and had tried to lure them to disaster? If so, then it wasn't just trying to kill Tamzin, but Alec and Moonlight as well . . .

She got to her feet and went to Moonlight. He lowered his head and nuzzled her as she put her arms around his neck, hugging him. When she looked over her shoulder, she saw that Alec had stood up, too. He was staring at Moonlight with a strange, respectful look, almost as if he was in awe.

'I know that animals are supposed to have a sixth sense,' he said slowly, 'but I've never believed it. Now, though . . .'

'Yes,' said Tamzin. 'I know.' She paused. 'Moonlight's very special. And he's a good friend to me.'

Alec didn't answer, but held out a hand to Moonlight. Moonlight snuffled at his fingers, clearly trusting him – and suddenly Tamzin had an overwhelming urge to confide in Alec. She needed help. And what had just happened proved to her that Alec was an ally and not an enemy.

She said shyly, 'Alec . . . there's something I want to tell you. And I want to ask for your help.'

He looked at her. 'Of course, Tamzin. Anything I can do – especially now.'

She nodded, and bit her lip. This wasn't going to be easy, but . . .

'All right.' She took a deep breath, and Moonlight whickered as though he was encouraging her. 'Have you ever heard the legend of the Grey Horse . . .?'

chapter four

Alec Brewer looked at Tamzin and said, 'Do you believe that the legend is true? That the Grey Horse and the Blue Horse really exist?'

'Yes!' Tamzin replied. 'I *know* they do!' She looked up at him. 'But you don't, do you?'

They had started back along the cliff path, Tamzin leading Moonlight and Alec walking beside her. Alec sighed. 'Tamzin, I don't want to sound like a stodgy grown-up. But the idea of good and evil spirits being real . . . honestly, I don't think it's possible.'

It could have been worse, Tamzin told

herself. At least he hadn't laughed at her. But Alec obviously did not believe in the super-natural. He thought that she was making it up; or at least, that she had heard an old story and let her imagination run away with her.

She didn't speak, and at last Alec said, 'Look, I don't want to be unkind. But it *is* a pretty far-fetched tale, isn't it? I mean, have you ever actually *seen* this Grey Horse?'

'Yes,' said Tamzin. 'Twice.'

He was obviously surprised by her answer, and she told him about the terrifying night when the Grey Horse had cornered her in the cave and the incoming tide had almost drowned her. She also told him about the confrontation on the clifftop, when the Grey Horse had tried to drive her over the edge.

'Both times it nearly killed me,' she finished. 'But Moonlight saved my life. Just like he saved us both today.' And silently she added to herself, *Oh, yes; he* is *special. I feel safe when he's near me; as if he's looking out*

for me somehow. But I can't explain that to
anyone else.

Alec had listened seriously to her story, but now he shook his head. 'Honestly, Tamzin, I'm still not convinced,' he said. 'Look: what happened this morning can easily be explained. It was a simple case of Moonlight's animal senses coming to the rescue. And the other things that happened to you – well, I'm sure they can be explained in the same way. Getting cut off by the tide; being run away with by a bolting horse – you must have been terrified! So it's not surprising that your imagination got overloaded. You *thought* you saw the Grey Horse. But it was just a sort of waking dream. It wasn't real.'

'Joel used to think that,' said Tamzin unhappily.

'Your friend who was riding with you on the beach?'

She nodded. 'His parents run a riding stable near here. Moonlight's one of their ponies.'

She blinked. 'He *used* to think it, but he doesn't any more. Because he's seen the Grey Horse, too.'

Alec thought for a few moments, then said, 'Listen, Tamzin, there's no point in us arguing about this. You believe in the Grey Horse, and I don't. But I'm interested in the story, so how about if I see what else I can find out about the legend?'

Tamzin brightened. 'Would you?'

'Certainly. It'll fit in with my investigations here. And if you want to help me, you're very welcome.'

'I'd like that,' she said.

'Then it's a deal!' They were coming to the place where the cliff path joined the track through the valley, and Alec added, 'I'm not going to do any more work today, mind you. I'm still pretty shaken after that scare, and I expect you are, too.' He rubbed his arm and grinned ruefully. 'And this is aching a bit, where Moonlight grabbed me! So I'll say goodbye. I've got your nan's phone number, and I'll let you know whatever I find out.'

He gave Moonlight a pat and walked away towards the beach, where his car was parked. Tamzin watched him go. She was disappointed that he had not believed her, but though his attitude was not what she had hoped, it was better than she had feared. Even if he didn't believe, at least he was willing to help her.

Alec was out of sight now, so she gathered up Moonlight's reins, put one foot in a stirrup and swung herself into the saddle. She *was* still shaken, and starting to feel cold. She would go back to the stables, she thought. Then when Joel returned, she could tell him what had happened.

Moonlight was much calmer on the way back, though Tamzin could feel some left-over tension through the reins, and every now and then he tossed his head, jingling the bit in his mouth. At the stables she unsaddled him and rubbed him down, then gave him more carrot chunks than she should have done as a special thank you. Joel and the trekking party still weren't back, so she cleaned tack while she waited for them. It was past noon when she heard the clatter of hooves in the yard, and then Mrs Richards insisted that they should all have a proper lunch in the house. So it wasn't until the afternoon that she had the chance to talk to Joel alone.

She thought he would agree with her that, despite the danger, the incident with Alec had proved that he was not an enemy. But she was wrong.

'Tam, are you crazy?' Joel exploded. 'It was a totally stupid thing to do, going up there on your own! And it hasn't proved anything at all!'

'What do you mean?' She was dismayed.

'Look,' said Joel, 'how do you *know* that Moonlight was trying to save Alec Brewer? He might have been trying to stop Alec pulling you *all* down with the landslide!'

'Oh, Joel, that's ridiculous!' Tamzin argued. 'I was there; I saw it!'

But it was no use; Joel just wouldn't be convinced. They didn't quarrel, but neither of them could persuade the other, and eventually they agreed to call a truce. They thought differently; that was all there was to it.

'But you've got to be careful,' Joel said darkly. 'Promise me!'

'Of course. I promise.'

They left it at that. But before going home, Tamzin went to Moonlight's box to say goodbye.

'*You* trust Alec, don't you?' she whispered to the pony. 'I know you do. You saved his life. How did you know, Moonlight? How did you know what was going to happen?'

Moonlight whickered gently and nuzzled her, his mane tickling her face. He seemed to understand what she was saying to him. She had always known that Moonlight was special. But now a new thought had come to her. Could Moonlight be linked with the benevolent spirit of the Blue Horse? After what had happened today, she couldn't help wondering . . .

Nan had finished repairing the picture frame, and the following afternoon she and Tamzin were re-hanging the painting in Tamzin's room when the phone rang.

'I'll get it,' Nan said. She went out, and Tamzin stood gazing at the picture. The galloping blue-white horse was very like Moonlight; yet Nan had painted it a long time ago, before she had ever seen him. Was that significant?

Tamzin was still thinking about that when Nan returned.

'That was Alec,' she said. 'He was on his mobile, calling from the beach. He's found something interesting, and he'd like us to go and look at it.'

* * *

'Oh!' Tamzin's eyes lit up and she forgot about the painting. 'Can we, Nan?'

'Yes, of course. Get your jacket; we'll walk straight down there.'

The tide was out, and there was a family party on the beach, but they were just sitting on the rocks in the sunshine and watching the sea. Round the headland, Tamzin and Nan found Alec alone at the blocked cave entrance. More rubble had come down in yesterday's landslip, and the sea had scattered it widely on the beach.

'The tide's moved some of the boulders over the cave mouth, too,' Alec said as they all looked at the rubble. 'There's a gap there now; see it?' He pointed, and Tamzin and Nan stared. There *was* a gap, but it was no more than a narrow slit between two of the fallen rocks.

'It's too small for anyone to get through,' said Nan.

'I know,' Alec agreed. 'It's very frustrating.

However, there's some good news, because
I found these.'

He showed them several pieces of broken
stone. They were strangely smooth and even,
and their edges were sharply regular.

Nan peered at them. 'What peculiar
shapes they are,' she said. 'They don't look
natural.'

'I don't think they are natural,' Alec agreed.
'I think they've been carved. And that's not
the only odd thing about them. They're a
different kind of stone to anything I've seen
in these cliffs. I'm sure they were brought
here from somewhere further away.'

Tamzin was peering at the fragments, too,
and something inside her seemed to turn over
with a lurch. 'Nan . . .' she said softly, 'this
stone . . . it looks just like –' She stopped
abruptly.

'Yes,' said Nan. 'It does.'

They were both thinking the same thing.
The colours and patterns in these pieces were

familiar. They were the same kind of stone from which the statue of the Grey Horse had been carved.

Alec had seen their expressions, and was puzzled. 'What's wrong?' he asked. 'Do you know something about these?'

'Yes,' Nan replied. 'I believe we do.' She hesitated, as if she was uncertain. Then she made a decision.

'I think you'd better come back to Chapel Cottage, Alec,' she said, 'and I'll explain.'

On the way back Alec was agog with curiosity, but Nan refused to tell him anything. At the house, Tamzin was surprised when Nan fetched a trowel and went out into the garden. For a minute she couldn't believe what Nan was going to do – but when Nan crouched down and began to dig in a certain spot, there could be no doubt of it.

As the buried sack was revealed, Tamzin felt a surge of sick fright, and awful memories

flooded into her mind. In that bag were the
pieces of the statue she had broken – the
statue of the Grey Horse. It wasn't complete,
for in a rash, angry moment she had thrown
one piece into the sea. So the statue could
not be properly repaired, and that had added
strength to the curse it carried. Nan had made
the best she could of it; she had buried the
pieces in an effort to protect Tamzin. But
now they were to see the light of day again.
Would anything happen? Would there be a
sudden screaming gale, a bolt of lightning out
of nowhere, a second earth tremor?

Nothing did happen, and with an effort
Tamzin got a grip on her nerves. Nan came
back into the kitchen, carrying the sack. She
put it on the table, opened it and took out
several of the statue fragments.

'You're the expert, Alec,' she said. 'Are
these the same kind of stone as the pieces you
found on the beach?'

Alec picked up a fragment and studied it

carefully. He compared it with his own pieces, and gave an excited gasp.

'It *is* the same! Where on earth did these come from?'

'Tamzin,' said Nan, 'put the kettle on, will you? I'm going to make some tea. And then . . .' She looked at Tamzin very intently. 'I'd like to talk to Alec alone. Would you mind very much?'

Tamzin's face fell. Whatever was going to be said, she wanted to hear it. She opened her mouth to protest – but stopped abruptly as an idea occurred to her.

'All right.' She paused. 'Is it OK if I go down to the beach again?'

'Yes, that's fine,' said Nan. 'But keep an eye on the tide, won't you? It'll be coming in now.'

When Tamzin passed the kitchen window on her way to the garden gate, she could see Nan and Alec sitting at the table. They were talking intently; Tamzin couldn't hear

* * *

what was being said, but the rest of the statue fragments were spread out between them.

She went through the gate and hurried along the valley path. There would still be time to get round the headland before the tide reached it, and she badly wanted to take another look around the cave entrance. Alec's discovery had excited her. If his pieces *were* of the same stone as the Grey Horse's statue, was it possible that she might find the one missing piece that could make the statue complete again?

The family party had gone, and the beach was deserted. Tamzin jumped the stream and ran round the jutting rocks to the cave, where she started to search among the debris. But after ten minutes' feverish hunting, she straightened up and reluctantly faced the truth. Of course the missing piece wasn't here. How could it be? She had thrown it into the sea, months ago, when the statue was first broken. It was gone, washed away, lost. It couldn't possibly reappear among the rubble of a rockfall.

Suddenly she was angry with herself for being so stupid. There was no point in this. She might as well go back to Chapel Cottage.

She turned, then paused, gazing at the blocked cave mouth. The gap Alec had pointed out earlier was dead ahead of her, reachable over tumbled boulders. It certainly was narrow; as Nan had said, no one could get through it.

Or at least . . .

Tamzin peered harder, narrowing her eyes, and her heart began to thump with excitement. An adult couldn't make it through the gap. But she could. And a new, wild idea began to take shape in her mind . . .

She ran to the foot of the piled boulders and began to scramble over them. She didn't even think about the incoming tide; the only thought in her head was to get through the gap and into the cave, to see what was there.

She *had* to do it. It was a need, a compulsion; nothing else mattered.

She reached the gap, started to squeeze herself in –

And a voice said clearly, '*NO!*'

Tamzin jumped, nearly losing her balance on the rock. She spun round, expecting to see someone on the sand behind her – but there was nobody there. Only the sea . . . and she realized with a shock that the tide's edge was a mere few metres away.

A wave broke and sunlight glittered on its crest, dazzling her. Then the crest seemed to separate from the wave and become something else – *a white horse, galloping out of the sea –*

Tamzin blinked, shaking her head violently, and the vision vanished and was just an ordinary wave again. But for one moment she had seen the horse clearly. And she had recognized it without any shadow of doubt.

It was Moonlight.

chapter five

Tamzin stood frozen on the rock, staring at the place where the vision had appeared. It *was* Moonlight, she had absolutely no doubt of it. For one instant he had been there, as real to her as she was; then a moment later he was gone. But she had heard the warning voice, and it had stopped her from doing something very foolish and dangerous. She would have gone through the gap, forgetting everything but the overwhelming desire to get into the cave. And the tide was coming in.

But the voice had broken the spell . . .

* * *

Suddenly she didn't want to stay a moment longer. She jumped down from the rock and ran, pelting back the way she had come. As she raced round the headland the sea was almost licking at her feet.

Alec was walking down the beach towards her. He raised a hand and waved, and Tamzin hurried to meet him.

'Your nan said I'd find you here.' He smiled at her, but his eyes were serious. 'She told me the full story; about the broken statue, and why she buried the pieces. She also told me about the warning inscribed on the statue's base. And she showed me the full translation written down in her old family bible.'

Tamzin's breath caught in her throat, but she didn't speak. Alec went on.

'I'm starting to understand properly now, Tamzin. And I'd like to help you in any way I can.' They started to walk back. 'Those pieces of stone that I found,' Alec continued, 'I think they might possibly have been carved by the same person who made the Grey Horse statue.'

Tamzin was astonished. 'How can you tell?' she asked eagerly.

'I can't, not for sure. But the way they've been cut is very similar to the fragments your nan showed me. Not only that, but several of them are obviously parts of a horse carving. I think they might have been practice pieces for the statue. And that shows how important it was for the sculptor to get his statue absolutely right.'

Tamzin's heart was bumping. 'If they were in the cave before the rockfall, how could they have got here?' she wanted to know.

'Ah, that's still a mystery. There's some evidence that there was a settlement – like a village but much smaller – in the valley, many centuries ago. If your ancestors lived there, perhaps they also made the old mining tunnels inside these cliffs. And perhaps that particular cave had some special meaning for them; something religious, or superstitious.'

Tamzin looked up at him and said, 'So do you believe in the Grey Horse now?'

Alec hesitated. Then, to her disappointment, he replied, 'No. I'm sorry, but I still don't think it really exists. But,' he added as she was about to protest, 'the important thing is, your ancestors *did* believe in it, and so do you.' He smiled kindly. 'So if we can solve the mystery once and for all, it will put your mind at rest – and give me some very valuable help with my own work!'

Tamzin nodded. Behind them she heard a deep roar as an especially big wave broke. The noise of the sea was growing louder; it was growling now, and the wind was rising, too, blowing her hair around her face. She stopped and looked over her shoulder. There were choppy white wave crests right out to the horizon, and surf was surging against the great bulk of Lion Rock in the distance.

'The lion's roaring,' she said.

'The lion?' Alec looked puzzled, and she smiled, pointing out to sea.

'People call that Lion Rock,' she told him, 'and when the sea gets rough they say that the noise it makes is the lion roaring.' They walked on, and she added, 'It's a funny name for the rock. I mean, it doesn't look the least bit like a lion, does it?'

'No, it doesn't,' Alec agreed. 'Though of course "lion" might not be its proper name. It could be a corruption of an old Cornish word that means something completely different.'

That had never occurred to Tamzin, and she was intrigued.

'I don't know much Cornish,' said Alec, 'and I can't think of a word that sounds at all like "lion". But I'll do some research and see what I can find out. In the meantime, though, I need to find a way to get into that cave! That second landslip has made it much too risky to try again from the top, so the beach entrance is my only chance.' He sighed. 'I just wish I could get through!'

Tamzin said, 'Wishes come true, sometimes.'

Her own words startled her. That wasn't at all what she had meant to say! She had been about to tell Alec about the gap she had discovered, but the words had come out of nowhere, and she had spoken them without even thinking.

Quickly she looked back at the sea. Would she see the vision again; the form of Moonlight galloping among the breakers? But cloud had covered the sun and the water no longer dazzled her. The vision was not there.

Alec was striding on, unaware that anything strange had happened. But Tamzin was certain that *something* had made her say what she did.

And she believed there was a good reason.

*

* * *

'The weather's changing,' said Nan. 'I can smell it.'

Dusk was falling and she was closing the sitting-room curtains before she and Tamzin settled down to a game of Scrabble.

Tamzin looked up from arranging the board and letters. 'It's windy out,' she said. 'I got blown home from the beach earlier.'

'I'm not surprised. It's full moon, too, so there'll be a very big tide.' Nan gave the curtains a shake to straighten them and came to join Tamzin at the table. 'Not the sort of night to be out in a boat! Never mind; we're snug and safe. Now, whose turn is it to go first?'

In bed that night Tamzin could hear the sea. The lion really was roaring; the tide must be enormous, she thought, and the gusting wind blowing from seaward would drive it even higher. As Nan had said, she was glad to be safe in the house, warm under her duvet. And the painting, now restored to its place on her bedroom wall, gave her extra comfort.

By morning it was still windy and the weather forecast was predicting rain later. Tamzin went to the stables as usual, and she and Joel resigned themselves to the weekly task of cleaning all the metal parts of the horses' tack – stirrup irons, bits and buckles. They talked as they worked, and Tamzin told Joel about Alec's discovery of the stone fragments, and about the gap in the boulders covering the cave entrance. But she was reluctant to say anything about the compulsion that had almost made her go into the cave, or the voice and the vision that had made her stop. It would only start him worrying again, and she didn't want to set off another argument. So she left that part of the story untold.

It wasn't until mid-afternoon that they finished their cleaning job and had the chance to go riding.

'We'd better make it quick,' Joel said as

they emerged from the tack room. 'Look at that sky.'

Heavy cloud was gathering from the south-west, promising a downpour before very long. The weather forecast had been right.

'How about the beach, then?' Tamzin suggested. 'The tide's low enough for a canter, and we can get back faster than if we go on the cliffs.'

'Good idea. We'll take Sally-Ann and Mischa; they haven't been out for a while.'

They saddled up and trotted away along the valley path, Joel leading on the chestnut mare Mischa. Mischa was one of the biggest horses in the Richardses' stable. She towered over bay Sally-Ann; really she was far too big for Joel, but she had such a gentle temperament that, as Mrs Richards said, you could put a six-year-old beginner on her back without worrying. Tamzin followed on Sally-Ann. She wished she could have ridden Moonlight, but reminded herself that she didn't own him and couldn't expect him always to be available. Sally-Ann was a lovely pony, and riding was riding, after all.

There were a few cars in the car park, but most of the people on the beach were packing up and getting ready to leave before the rain arrived. A dog barked furiously at the two horses, and Sally-Ann shied, but Tamzin soon had her under control again and they headed for the firmer sand beyond the headland.

'Let's ride the whole beach, end to end, then back home,' said Joel.

'OK,' said Tamzin. 'But I'm not even going to *try* to race Mischa!'

He laughed, turned Mischa to the right and they gave the horses their heads. Mischa took off at once, her big hooves leaving deep prints as she broke into a canter. Tamzin held back for a few moments, watching the mare admiringly and wishing that she could ride as well as Joel. Sally-Ann shook her head and pawed the sand impatiently, wanting to follow.

* * *

'All right,' Tamzin said to her. 'Come on, then. But we won't catch them!'

She slackened her reins, and they were away.

They cantered to the far end of the beach, then galloped back the whole length of it, right to left. It was an exhilarating ride, with the wind in their faces and the pounding of the horses' hooves mingling with the pounding of the surf. Tamzin pretended that the beach was a great desert, and she was a tribal princess of ancient times, racing her pure-bred Arabian steed across the endless landscape. Or maybe she was an Ancient Briton, mounted on a wild pony that she had captured and tamed herself –

'Whoa!' She heard Joel's shout, and snapped out of her fantasy in time to see that they were almost at the end of the beach. She dropped her hands, reining Sally-Ann in, and they came to a halt near a rock outcrop where the turning tide was just beginning to swirl.

* * *

'Wow!' Joel was grinning broadly. 'That was great!'

Tamzin nodded breathless agreement, grinning back. The horses were excited too, dancing and snorting as they splashed in the shallows at the sea's edge.

'Better not hang around,' said Joel. 'The sky's starting to look really grim, and we don't want to get soaked. Come on; if we start back now, we should beat the rain home.'

They turned their horses and set off again, at a trot this time. Joel was ahead of Tamzin, but as they neared the headland he held Mischa back until she caught up, and said, 'Did you know horses love swimming? In the summer, Mum and Dad and I sometimes take them in the sea. We wear swimming gear and ride bareback. It's brilliant – you can come with us this year.'

He expected Tamzin to answer, but she didn't. She was staring towards the blocked cave, and she clearly had not heard a word he said.

'Tam? Hey, Tam! I said – '

Tamzin interrupted him. 'Joel, look! The boulders have moved.'

'Uh?'

'At the cave mouth. Remember I told you about the gap I found? Well, it's bigger now. Anyone could get through.'

'Oh, yes.' Joel saw it for himself. 'I see what you mean.'

'Nan said there was a really big tide last night,' Tamzin went on. 'It must have been powerful enough to shift that enormous rock. Alec's wish has come true . . .'

Joel looked at her sharply. 'What wish?'

Of course; she hadn't told him that part of yesterday's story. For a moment Tamzin hesitated, then suddenly she decided to be completely honest. Joel couldn't argue with her now. Not after this.

So, as they rode on, she told him the

* * *

details she had left out earlier: the compulsion, the voice, the vision of the galloping horse that she was certain had been Moonlight. Then the meeting with Alec, the wish he had made, and the words that had come to her seemingly from nowhere. *Wishes come true, sometimes.*

'It's as if something *told* me what was going to happen,' she said. 'And now, today, the gap's wide enough for Alec to get into the cave. The Blue Horse has done this, Joel; I'm sure of it! And it's a sign that Alec can be trusted!'

Joel didn't reply at first. In another minute or so they would reach the valley path. They would have to ride in single file then, making talking difficult, and Tamzin seethed with impatience as she waited for him to speak. Then abruptly he halted Mischa and turned to look at Tamzin.

'All right,' he said decisively. 'It sounds convincing; I can't argue with that any more.

And it might mean that the Blue Horse is getting stronger.' He smiled. 'Nothing quite like this has ever happened before, has it?'

She smiled back. 'No, it hasn't!'

'Mind you, if the Blue Horse *is* gaining strength, the Grey Horse isn't going to like it one bit. It'll fight back. It'll try harder to hurt you. So I still think we've got to be careful and stay alert.'

Tamzin saw the sense in that. The Grey Horse *would* fight. It would be angry. And that meant it was doubly dangerous.

Overhead, the sky was the colour of slate now. The daylight looked old and grim, as if something invisible had cast a vast shadow over the whole world. Tamzin looked down at her hands, which were clenched and tense on Sally-Ann's reins.

'You're right,' she said soberly. 'I'll watch out. Every step of the way.'

chapter six

Joel left Tamzin at the gate of Chapel Cottage and took both the horses on alone to the stables. It was just as well he did, for she hadn't been in the house more than fifteen minutes before the rain started.

'What a day!' said Nan, peering through the kitchen window. 'Typical springtime – though I must say we seem to be having much more than our fair share this year.'

Tamzin joined her at the window, but water was streaming down the glass in rivers, blurring the view of the world outside. Even here on the ground floor the noise of rain hammering on the roof was like a drum roll.

'I hope Joel got back before it started,' said Tamzin.

'Oh, he'll be home and dry by now,' Nan assured her. 'But I'm afraid there probably won't be any riding for you two tomorrow. The weather forecast says this is setting in for the night – everything'll be knee-deep in mud by morning.'

She was more right than she knew. The rain continued not only through that night but into the next day, and for two more days after that. Going to the stables was out of the question. The rain did slacken off to a drizzle now and then, but the breaks never lasted long enough for Tamzin to make her way up the valley without risking a complete soaking. Joel, phoning on his mobile, sounded increasingly gloomy. The horses were all restless and tetchy from lack of exercise, he said; at this rate the school holidays would be over before they had a chance to go riding again.

Apart from a quick shopping trip to the village by car, Tamzin and Nan did not venture out. It wasn't a lot of fun being stuck indoors. Nan needed to finish a commissioned painting, so Tamzin had to amuse herself for much of the time. Television was almost unwatchable because of interference caused by the weather, so instead she listened to the radio. There was a lot of weather talk on the local station. Apparently, the heavy rain was not widespread, but was concentrated just on this small area of Cornwall, while everywhere else remained relatively dry. Tamzin remembered Joel's warning about the Grey Horse, and tried not to feel uneasy.

Then, after three days and nights almost without a break, the fourth afternoon brought a real cloudburst. Nan was working in her studio, and Tamzin was getting tea ready when she heard an increasing noise, almost a roar, outside. Baggins sat up on his chair, ears flicking forward and eyes round and wide,

* * *

and when Tamzin looked out of the window she saw that the outside world was blotted out by a solid grey wall of water.

Nan came in a minute later.

'Just *look* at it!' she said in dismay. 'We haven't had a downpour like this in ages. My poor garden – all the spring flowers will be drowned!'

'Will we get flooded, do you think?' Tamzin asked worriedly.

'No, we should be all right; we're on a slope, so the surface water should run past us and into the bottom of the valley.' Nan turned the hot tap on and started to wash her hands. 'Mind you, some people probably will have problems. The land's already saturated, you see. It can't soak up any more, and all this new rain has to go somewhere. Let's just hope it doesn't last too long.'

But it did. All that night the rain drummed on the roof of Chapel Cottage, so that Tamzin's dreams were filled with the noise of it. She woke up several times, and lay listening to the falling water as it hissed on the ground and gurgled in the gutters and splashed on the overflowing water butt below her window. When dawn broke, though, the sounds began to ease off, and as full daylight came there was a sudden, extraordinary silence.

Tamzin scrambled out of bed and went to her window. She couldn't see anything, for the glass was misted over, so she opened the casement and looked out.

The sky was still heavy with grey clouds, but the rain had stopped, and the whole world gleamed wetly. Water dripped everywhere; from the roof, the window sills and every plant in the garden, and the grass was silvery with millions of droplets. But the rain had actually *stopped*.

There was a wonderful smell in the air; a kind of green scent, fresh and heady. Tamzin breathed it in deeply. She thought she could hear water running somewhere, but maybe it was just part of the general dripping sound. She didn't feel like going back to bed now, so she got dressed and went downstairs. Nan came down soon afterwards, and they had breakfast with the back door standing wide open and the fresh outdoor smell filling the kitchen. Only Baggins was not happy. He did venture outside, but was back in again in moments, shaking his paws and complaining about the wet with a cross 'Miaow!'

'I hope the Richardses are all right,' said Nan. 'Their land's in a bit of a hollow; with this much water around, they might have some problems. Maybe we'd better ring and find out.'

Tamzin called Joel, and was relieved to hear his news.

'We're OK so far,' he said. 'But if we get much more rain, Dad reckons we could be in trouble. There's quite a bit of flooding in the village already – two people have rung up to cancel rides because they can't get out of

76

their homes. Look,' he added, 'you'd better not come up to the stables today. It's far too wet underfoot for riding, let alone walking, and we'll be spending most of the day sweeping puddles out of the yard. I'll call you later, OK?'

'OK. But if you want any help –'

'You'll be the first person to know! See you.'

Tamzin tried not to feel too disappointed as she pulled on her Wellingtons and went to help Nan in the garden. They were trying to straighten some of the rain-battered plants when they heard the sound of an engine, and a familiar car came bumping and rocking down the rough lane to the house.

'It's Alec,' said Nan. 'He's in a hurry! Has something happened?'

The car slithered to a stop and Alec jumped out. His eyes were alight and he seemed breathless. 'Good morning!' he greeted them. 'Though I don't somehow think "good" is the right word! There are floods in the village; did you know? And part of the main road to Truro's under water; cars are having to go round the long way. But I've got some exciting news. I've just come from the beach – and I've been inside the cave!'

'The boulders!' Tamzin's eyes lit up, too. 'So the gap *is* big enough now!'

'It certainly is. I couldn't wait to come and tell you both. And I want to show you what I've found!'

They all piled into Alec's car and set off back to the beach. The tide was a long way out; it had turned, but Nan judged that they would have the best part of an hour to see Alec's discovery.

'I came at dawn, as soon as the rain stopped,' Alec explained eagerly, as they hurried towards the headland. 'I could hardly believe my eyes when I saw that it was possible to get into the cave!' He grinned at

Tamzin. 'You were right, you know. Wishes *do* come true sometimes.'

'Yes,' replied Tamzin, but she did not say any more.

The sea was very calm, the breakers flattened by the rain to small, murmuring wavelets. At the cave they all clambered carefully over the rocks to where the gap between the boulders showed dark and gaping.

Alec produced a powerful flashlight and eased himself into the dark hole. 'There's a bit of a drop on the other side, so I'll go through first and shine the torch for you.'

There was water running out of the cave, Tamzin noticed; quite a stream, in fact, splashing over the rocks and across the sand towards the sea. Alec disappeared, then after a few seconds his voice came back, echoing hollowly. 'All right, come on through. I'll light the way.'

With Nan right behind her and her heart

* * *

thumping with excitement, Tamzin slipped through the gap. Her boots splashed in water, then Alec's torch lit up the inside of the cave.

'There you go,' he said, grasping her hand to steady her as she jumped down on to wet sand. 'Stay there and I'll help your nan. All right, Isobel? Good! Right, all safe and sound.'

Nan emerged and she and Tamzin gazed around. Tamzin's first thought was that the cave looked very different from the last time she had seen it, before the rockfall. Memories of that night came back to her, and with a shudder she moved closer to Nan. She wondered suddenly if she should have come back here at all. But somehow, with Nan and Alec close by, she did not feel frightened, only curious.

'This way.' Alec pointed the flashlight towards the back of the cave. More images sprang into Tamzin's mind: there had been a shallow pool there, with rocks behind it, and above the rocks was a long, narrow fissure.

And wedged in the fissure, she had found the first piece of her blue glass talisman . . .

The pool was there, and the rocks. Tamzin's breath caught in her throat as she looked up, half expecting to see again the strange, pale glow that had led her to the talisman. But the fissure was gone. Instead, she found herself staring in amazement at the mouth of a wide tunnel.

Alec heard her gasp, though he didn't understand the reason for it.

'I can't be sure,' he said, 'but I *think* the earth tremor opened this tunnel up. Of course, I hadn't been in here before, so –'

Tamzin interrupted him. 'It did,' she said. 'There was just a narrow slit in the rocks. I remember it.' She felt Nan's fingers close round hers and squeeze reassuringly. She squeezed back, grateful.

'Have you been into the tunnel?' Nan asked Alec.

'Oh, yes. I went in about twenty metres before I came to tell you about it. And it isn't a natural tunnel; at least, not all of it. It's been cut out of the rock. I'd say that it was made many, many centuries ago.' He shone the flashlight on the tunnel entrance, and added, 'What really puzzles me, though, is *why* the tunnel was made.'

'Perhaps it was an adit?' Nan suggested. 'You know; an air tunnel, joining up with one of the old mine shafts?'

'That's what I thought, at first. But who would dig an air tunnel that filled with water at every high tide? It doesn't make sense.'

'I see what you mean,' said Nan. 'And for the same reason, it can't have been an entrance or exit way for miners.'

'Yet someone obviously wanted to be able to get to the beach at particular times – and, I wouldn't mind betting, for a particular purpose.' Alec looked back at the gap through which they had come. 'How long do you think we've got before we need to worry about the tide?'

Nan checked her watch by the torchlight. 'Half an hour,' she said. 'No more.'

'Right. Then there's time for me to show you something I found inside the tunnel – if you don't mind a paddle and a climb?'

Nan laughed. 'I'm not too old yet! Tamzin? Is that all right for you?'

Tamzin hesitated. She, too, was looking back at the gap in the boulders. Daylight showed through it; the sea was hidden from sight, but she could hear its restless murmur, amplified by the cave and echoing like a sighing voice. She thought of the tide; she remembered her last, terrifying experience here . . . But Nan and Alec were with her now. There was nothing to be afraid of.

So why did she feel a sense of dread creeping up on her?

* * *

She shook the feeling off, suddenly angry with herself. *Chicken*, she thought. *It's perfectly safe. It is!*

She said aloud, 'Yes. It's fine.'

With Alec in the lead, the three of them waded through the shallow pool and climbed up the gently sloping rocks on the far side. The tunnel entrance was like an open mouth in front of them. Alec went in first, the torchlight bobbing. Again, Tamzin looked over her shoulder. The cave was dark but empty. Nothing moved; nothing was forming out of the shadows to menace them. It was *perfectly* all right.

Gathering up her nerve, she ducked into the tunnel.

chapter seven

The tunnel sloped upwards, not too steeply but enough to make the climb hard work. The roof was only just high enough for Nan to stand upright; Alec, though, had to bend. As they ventured further in, Tamzin saw that the walls to either side were not a natural shape but had obviously been cut. That must have been what Alec meant when he said the passage was man-made.

Then, ahead of her, the bobbing beam of light stopped moving for a moment before Alec raised the torch and shone it on the wall.

* * *

'This is what I *really* want you to see,' he told them. 'Just there, in the middle of the light.'

Tamzin and Nan craned to look. There, on an unusually smooth patch of wall, a lot of marks of some kind had been carved or scratched into the rock.

'They look as if they were made by a chisel,' said Nan.

'I think they were,' Alec agreed. 'But look closely. They're very worn, but don't you think they look like letters?'

'Oh, yes!' Nan exclaimed. 'I can see them now. The words aren't English, though, are they?'

'No. They're Cornish. I wasn't sure at first, but then I came across this . . .'

He swung the torch to another part of the wall. Tamzin peered more closely – and gasped.

'Nan, *look*!'

The letters were broken and uneven. But

four words could be read. Tamzin had seen
those words before.

They said: *Gweetho An Men Ma*. The same
words that had been carved on the base of the
Grey Horse statue.

Nan said, '*Oh . . .*' very softly.

'They mean: "Guard this stone", don't
they?' said Alec. 'The first words of the rhyme
that's translated in your family bible.'

The complete rhyme ran through Tamzin's
mind then, and she shivered.

Guard this stone that prisons me,
For if it should be cast away,
Then I shall come from surging sea,
And turn your world to stormy grey.

It was the prophecy of the Grey Horse; a
warning to beware, and to protect the statue
that held the dark spirit captive. And here it
was, carved into the wall of an ancient tunnel
in the cliff.

'I think', said Alec, 'this tells us something
about the tunnel's purpose. There's a link with

the legend of the Grey Horse. But the question is, what *is* that link?'

'Have you been able to read any more words in the carvings?' Nan asked.

'A few. I wrote them down earlier, though I don't understand what they mean. They could be the rest of the rhyme. But I don't think they are, because they're carved on another part of the wall. I think they're something new to us. If we can translate them, they might give us a vital clue.'

'I agree,' said Nan, then checked her watch again. 'We'd better go, or the tide will creep up on us.' She paused, looking at Tamzin. 'Are you all right, pet?'

Tamzin nodded. Truthfully, though, she wasn't all right. She had got over her bout of nerves, but a new thought had occurred to her, and she didn't like it. What was it Joel had said? 'If the Blue Horse is gaining strength, the Grey Horse isn't going to like it one bit. It'll fight back.' She had feared that something unpleasant might happen in the tunnel; but nothing had. This was an ideal place for the Grey Horse to strike back at them, yet it had done nothing. *Why?* she asked herself. And the only answer she could come up with was: *Because it's planning something else. Something far, far worse.*

Suddenly she had to force back an overwhelming urge to run helter-skelter back to the tunnel entrance, through the pool and out of the cave as fast as she could. She battled against the feeling, but as they started back the way they had come she tried to make Nan and Alec walk more quickly. *Hurry, oh please, hurry, before something goes wrong!*

She could have shouted with sheer relief when they emerged from the tunnel and splashed through the pool to the sand. Daylight still showed between the boulders at the cave mouth – Tamzin had had an irrational terror that they would find the gap had closed, trapping them – and she scrambled up to the cleft and wriggled through into the open air.

Nothing horrific greeted her. The tide was closer but still a long way from cutting them off, and there were no monstrous waves or rolling storm clouds or any of the other things that she had feverishly imagined might be ready to pounce. Nan and Alec were following more slowly, and as she waited for them Tamzin looked out to sea.

Then, as she looked, she realized something. A mile or so out, Lion Rock towered from the sea . . . and it was *exactly* opposite the cave mouth. The two were lined up so precisely that Tamzin was astonished not to have noticed it before. But perhaps the thing that made her notice now was the new stream that ran from the cave. It flowed across the sand, straight as an arrow to the sea's edge. And straight as an arrow towards the rock.

It *meant* something. Tamzin was as sure of that as she had ever been of anything. The alignment of the cave and the rock, the unnatural straightness of the stream – they weren't coincidence. And now, the messages Alec had found. Messages carved inside the stone of the cliff, waiting down the centuries for someone to find and understand them. Slowly but surely, the threads of the ancient mystery were starting to weave together.

Tamzin scanned the horizon, where the sea met the sky. Dark clouds were gathering again, and the sight of them made her think of a cauldron beginning to bubble. Something *was* brewing; she was certain of it. But what?

She heard voices, and turned to see Nan and Alec climbing down the rocks from the cave entrance.

'Whew!' Nan was out of breath. 'Well, Alec, you really *have* set us a puzzle now!'

Alec smiled. 'Time for some research in the nearest library, I think,' he said. 'Just so long as the floods don't stop me getting there.'

'Talking of floods,' said Nan, 'I don't like

the look of that sky. Come on – let's hurry back to the car before we all get a drenching!'

The weather forecast that evening came as an unpleasant surprise. As if there hadn't already been more than enough rain, another downpour was expected tomorrow – and this time, it looked set to be truly colossal.

Tamzin listened to the broadcast with growing alarm. The announcer was talking of 'freak' conditions, and widespread flood warnings were out. Nan still said that Chapel Cottage would be safe, but Tamzin was finding that harder to believe. '*And turn your world to stormy grey . . .*' The words of the ancient rhyme ran through her head again and again. Was this the Grey Horse's doing? Was it the beginning of a new attack? The worst of the terrible weather was concentrated on this one small area, and she couldn't shake off the fear that *she* was its target.

Nan knew Tamzin was afraid, and knew

why. They didn't talk about it, though she put an arm round Tamzin's shoulders in a small, private gesture of comfort. Alec had rung before lunch, to say that he had managed to get to Redruth and was beginning his research in the Cornish Studies library there, but they hadn't heard from him again. They were both waiting anxiously for a second phone call. By nightfall, though, it had not come.

It drizzled that night, but nothing worse, and by morning the drizzle had stopped, though the sky was very ominous. Then, as Tamzin and Nan were about to sit down to breakfast, Tamzin's mobile rang.

It was Joel – and he sounded worried.

'We've just heard the latest weather forecast,' he said. 'It sounds like we're really in for it this time, and Dad reckons we're going to get flooded out for certain. Our fields aren't safe; we're going to have to move all the horses to higher ground. Can you come up here and help?'

* * *

As soon as she learned what Joel had said, Nan was on her feet. 'We'll both go,' she declared. 'I might not be much use with the horses, but I can help at the house and stables. The Richardses are going to need every pair of hands they can get!'

They hauled on Wellingtons and waterproofs, and hurried to Nan's car. The car was reluctant to start ('It's the wet,' Nan said. 'It gets into everything'), but eventually it coughed and spluttered into life and they set off.

As the road climbed up beside the valley and the land opened out, Tamzin was dismayed to see huge, still sheets of water covering all the lower-lying ground.

'I didn't know it was this bad!' she said to Nan, aghast.

'It'll be even worse further inland,' Nan told her. 'And if we get more later . . . well, it almost doesn't bear thinking about.'

The road route to the Richardses' was much

longer than the valley path, and by the time
the house and stables came in sight Tamzin
was keyed up with nervous impatience. Mrs
Richards was in the yard, and another car was
already there too.

'Oh, thank you so much, Mrs Weston!' Mrs
Richards said with relief when she heard that
Nan had come to help. 'We've got enough
people to cope with the horses, but there's the
house, too – we need to get as much ground-
floor furniture as we can upstairs.'

'That's what I thought,' said Nan. 'Tell me
what to do, and I'll get started.'

'Well, if you can help my husband indoors,
that leaves me free to be in charge of the horse
movers.'

Nan strode away towards the house, and
Tamzin and Mrs Richards ran to the stables
where Joel and two of the riding school's
regular customers were getting the horses
ready.

'Right!' said Mrs Richards. 'Luckily, a

farmer neighbour has offered to lend us a
barn and field on higher ground. The horses
will be safe there. It's four miles away by
road, but only two across country. So we'll
ride there by the shorter way, and everyone
will lead two more horses. If four of us go,
that's twelve horses at a time, so we can do
it in two journeys. Denise,' she added to one
of the customers, 'would you mind staying
here and seeing to the second batch of horses,
while the rest of us take the first?'

Denise, whom Tamzin had vaguely met
before, seemed quite relieved to be staying
rather than riding, so within a few minutes
Tamzin found herself mounted on Moonlight,
with Lark and stolid Pippin on leading reins
beside her. Joel rode Jester, Mrs Richards
was on piebald Dandy, and the other
customer, a middle-aged man, took the big
chestnut Mischa. The twelve horses stamped
and pawed, and the riders gathered up their
reins.

* * *

'All ready?' said Mrs Richards. 'Right – let's go. And hope the rain doesn't start before we've finished!'

chapter eight

The party headed into the valley and rode cautiously along the muddy, slippery path. Tamzin was third in the line – and before long she felt glad that she had two quiet ponies to lead. For Moonlight was misbehaving. He was skittish and restless, trying to trot when he should have walked, shaking his head and swishing his tail.

'Moonlight, stop it!' she told him. 'I know you've been stuck indoors for days, but you mustn't play up now!'

Moonlight snorted and shook his head again, so hard that he almost jerked the reins out of her hands. He laid his ears back, dancing, and Lark behind him whinnied a protest as one of his hind hooves kicked her.

'What's the matter with him?' Joel asked, looking over his shoulder.

'I don't know!' Tamzin called back. 'He was just like this on the cliffs the other day, when he saved us from the landslip! Moonlight, *no*! Calm down!'

But Moonlight would not calm down. All the way up the valley and along the track to the new field, he was almost impossible to control. Several times as he lurched or slithered Tamzin nearly fell off, and Lark and Pippin on their leading reins were catching his mood and becoming edgy, too. This behaviour, Tamzin knew, was more than just high spirits after being confined in the stable. To her, it seemed as if Moonlight was *angry* about something. Though what it could be was a mystery.

'If only you could talk!' she said, stroking

his neck in an effort to calm him, and gripping
tightly with her knees to stay in the saddle
as the pony pranced and fidgeted. 'Then you
could tell me what's wrong. Come on,
Moonlight; shh, steady. *Please!*'

She was thankful when the borrowed field
came in sight. The farmer was waiting for
them at the gate, and as the ponies streamed
through he said, 'Put them straight into the
barn, I would.' He pointed to a big timber
building on the far side of the field. 'No sense
in leaving 'em out to get wetter than they
have to.'

The field was already sodden with rain, and
plodding across it to the barn was hard work.
Even Moonlight was quieter – until, as they
approached the open barn doors, he suddenly
gave a shrill, squealing whinny and reared, his
forelegs raking the air. Tamzin dropped the
leading reins and made a grab for the saddle
pommel; somehow she stayed on Moonlight's
back, but as his hooves came down again with

a jarring thump she lost both stirrups and started to slide sideways. All she could do was make an undignified scramble to the ground as Moonlight reared a second time. Then Mrs Richards was there on Dandy, reaching out to catch hold of Moonlight's bridle.

'Whoa, Moonlight, whoa!' Moonlight tried to pull away but Mrs Richards held on. 'Are you all right, Tamzin?'

'Yes, I'm fine,' said Tamzin breathlessly. 'But Lark and Pippin –'

'Don't worry, Joel's got them. I think you'd better lead them in, and I'll look after Moonlight.'

Getting Moonlight into the barn was a struggle. He reared, kicked, pulled and protested, and only when the farmer, who was a big and powerful man, came to help did they finally manage to make him go inside.

'Better tie him up somewhere,' said Mrs Richards, 'or he'll try to kick his way out again, the mood he's in.'

Tamzin looked fearfully at Joel. 'Moonlight just isn't *like* that,' she said. 'Something's wrong, Joel. Something's *really* wrong!'

'Yes,' said Joel. 'But what? He can't tell us . . . Look, Tam, there's no way you can ride him back to collect the others. We'd better leave him here, and you take Lark.'

Tamzin saw the sense in that, though she wasn't at all happy. She was certain that Moonlight had a reason for not wanting to leave the stables. But what could that reason possibly be? If the promised downpour came, this place would be much safer than the Richardses'. So why hadn't he wanted to go?

Then a terrible thought occurred to her. Maybe *she* was the cause. Maybe Moonlight did not want to be separated from her, because he sensed that something dangerous was in the air. A new threat . . .

Mrs Richards had tied Moonlight up at the far end of the barn and was unsaddling him. The farmer had brought some bales of hay for the horses to eat, and most of them were already snatching mouthfuls and crunching them. But Moonlight wasn't interested in food. He stamped restlessly, his head swinging from side to side as far as his halter rope would allow. Then he saw Tamzin, and uttered a piercing whinny that echoed through the barn. Tamzin would have gone towards him, but Joel said, 'Tam, there isn't time! We've got to go back for the other horses. Come on; you can talk to him when we get back.'

Reluctantly she followed to where Mrs Richards was now buckling Moonlight's saddle on to Lark. The four riders left a few minutes later, slogging across the field. Though it wasn't yet lunchtime the sky was darkening, and Mrs Richards said, 'We'd better hurry if we're going to finish before the rain comes. It's too slippery to canter, but we can try a trot once we get on to the track.'

The ride back to the Richardses' took much

less time than the outward ride had done,
partly because there were no horses to lead,
but mostly because Moonlight was not there
to hold everyone up. Nan came out of the
house as they arrived, and reported that
everything except the heavy furniture was
now safely stowed upstairs. She had made
tea, and the riders gratefully drank mugs of
it before setting out again with the last of the
horses. Tamzin had only one pony to lead this
time, but though everything went smoothly,
the horses became more and more restless as
they rode on. Little wonder, Tamzin thought,
glancing uneasily at the sky. It was as dark as
a bruise now and looking more threatening
with every minute. The daylight was reduced
to gloom, so that it was hard to see the path,
and she could feel the beginning of rain in
the air.

They hurried on as fast as safety allowed –
then, just as they reached the field gate, the
heavens opened. The rain came down in a

roaring deluge that took everyone's breath away, and in the minute it took for them to reach the shelter of the barn they and the horses were drenched. The farmer was waiting for them, and as the last horse rushed in he hauled the doors shut against the weather's onslaught. Tamzin slid from Lark's back and started to unfasten the saddle girth.

'We'll have to rub them all down,' Joel shouted above the tremendous noise of rain hammering on the barn roof. But the farmer, overhearing, said, 'No time for that! If I'm going to drive you all back to the stables, we'll have to leave right now – half an hour of this and even my Land Rover won't get through! My daughter will look after the new horses, and I'll give her a hand when I come back. Hurry, now!'

'What about Moonlight?' In dismay Tamzin looked for him among the milling animals. But it was so gloomy in the barn that she couldn't see him.

'Don't worry, they're all here, safe and sound,' the farmer told her. 'Now come on!'

She had no choice but to go. They sprinted the few metres to where the Land Rover was parked, and huddled inside as the farmer drove slowly and cautiously away. The tarmac road was awash with streams that ran faster than the car, and when they reached the Richardses', Tamzin saw that the yard was already covered by a sheet of water.

Mr Richards came splashing to meet them, holding a huge umbrella over his head.

'Not that it's much use to you lot,' he said when he saw them. 'You're all soaked through anyway!'

Nan, too, was waiting, and she and Tamzin went home straight away. Everything in the house that could be moved was now upstairs, and all the horses' tack had been stowed in the stable loft.

'I'll ring you later!' Joel called over the noise of the downpour as Tamzin scrambled into

Nan's car. 'And don't worry about Moonlight. He'll be fine!'

She waved a hand to him. 'Good luck!'

Tamzin and Nan reached the rough lane that led to Chapel Cottage to find it turned to a racing brown river several centimetres deep. The car's engine had spluttered and coughed most of the way back, and as Nan turned it on to the level ground outside the house it gave a final wet stutter and died into silence. They ran for shelter, splashing through puddles that bubbled like cauldrons with the rain bouncing from their surfaces, and hurled themselves in at the kitchen door.

'Whew!' said Nan as they took off their sodden coats and hung them to drip in the porch. 'I've never seen rain like it!'

Tamzin pulled off her boots, which were so wet that she felt as if she was paddling. 'Are you *sure* we'll be all right here, Nan?' she asked worriedly.

'Oh, yes. You could see when we came in;

all the water's running past the house. We
might get a bit coming in under the tiles and
running down the walls, but nothing worse
than that.' Nan flicked the light switch, and
the kitchen filled with brightness. 'And we've
still got electricity; that's a relief! Go on, love;
go upstairs and change out of those wet
things. I'd have a nice hot bath, if I were you.'

'All right, Nan.' Tamzin smiled at her, and
tried not to listen to the clamour of the rain
as she squelched towards the stairs.

chapter nine

The rainstorm lasted nearly all night, and for most of the time Tamzin lay awake. She couldn't stop worrying about Moonlight. How was he now, two miles away in the farmer's barn? Was he still upset, or had he calmed down? And what had made him behave in the way he had?

She kept remembering her earlier fear: that a new danger was brewing, and Moonlight knew it and did not want to be separated from her. If so, then maybe he had a good reason – for Tamzin believed that this incredible rain was not natural. She felt sure that the Grey

Horse was behind it, and that it was concentrating its efforts on this area because she was here. Without Moonlight nearby to protect her, she was dangerously vulnerable.

She turned over in bed and gazed at Nan's painting. She couldn't see any detail of it in the darkness, but the shape of the blue-tinted horse was dimly visible. Not for the first time, Tamzin could almost believe that it was moving; the mane and tail blowing like mist, the head tossing, the slender legs galloping in the surf . . .

Tamzin's fingers closed round the glass talisman on her bracelet, and she whispered softly, '*Blue Horse . . . Blue Horse, tell Moonlight that I'm all right. Help him . . . and keep us safe, if you can!*'

Just for a moment the vague image of the horse in the painting seemed to become brighter and clearer. Then it faded back into the gloom, and she could no longer imagine that it was moving.

* * *

But outside, the sound of the rain began to ease. It was falling less heavily, not hammering now but just a gentle, swishing patter. The storm was passing. It was nearly over.

For now . . .

Tamzin went back to sleep for an hour or two. When she woke, daylight had come and the rain had stopped.

'Look,' Nan said when they went downstairs for breakfast, 'there's a little break in the clouds. We might even get some sunshine later on!' She filled the kettle. 'I wonder if the Richardses are all right? We'd better call them, and find out.'

Tamzin dialled the Richardses' house phone but it was out of order, so she rang Joel's mobile, and was relieved to hear his voice.

'We're OK,' he said. 'The water's nearly half a metre deep around the house and the stables, and the electricity's off. But we're camping upstairs, and we've got enough food to last us

*   *   *

for a few days. Dad reckons it won't be long before the flood goes down.'

'What about the horses?' Tamzin asked anxiously.

'We were just going to phone and check when you rang,' said Joel. 'But don't worry; they'll be fine where they are.'

'All the same, when you *do* know –'

'Sure, I'll tell you.' Joel laughed. 'They're probably enjoying the rest!'

Tamzin was reassured by his cheerful mood. But half an hour later, when her mobile rang, she had a shock.

'Tam . . .' Joel's voice was strained, and Tamzin knew instantly that something was wrong.

'What is it?' Her voice rose as an awful feeling of dread clutched at her stomach.

'Mum just talked to the farmer,' said Joel tensely. 'One of the horses is missing.' There was a long pause, and Tamzin *knew* what was coming. 'It's Moonlight.'

* * *

There could be no possible doubt, Joel told her. The farmer knew how many horses should have been in the barn, but when he counted them this morning, the number was one short. He remembered Moonlight in particular, because of the way he had behaved yesterday and because he was the only white or dapple grey the Richardses owned. Now, he was gone.

'He must have broken out somehow!' Tamzin said in distress.

'He didn't,' Joel told her. 'That's the weirdest thing. The barn door was barred on the outside till the farmer went in, and Moonlight didn't kick any planks out and escape that way. He's just vanished.' There was a long pause, then he added, 'Everyone else thinks he's been stolen. But I think we know different. Don't we?'

Tamzin's skin had turned ice cold, and her heart was beating very hard. 'Yes,' she whispered. 'I think we do.'

∗ ∗ ∗

Something was beginning. First the extraordinary rain; now Moonlight . . . the power of the Grey Horse was rising. And the thought of what might have become of her beloved pony made Tamzin feel sick with fear.

'We've got to search for him!' she said urgently.

'I agree,' said Joel. 'But right now I'd need a boat to even get out of the house. Until the water goes down, I can't do anything!'

'I can! We're not flooded here.'

'Right – but where to start? There are no clues, nothing at all.' He hesitated. 'He might be trying to get home, of course; in which case he could turn up here, or as near as he can get, at any moment. But if he's got lost, or . . .' Joel dropped his voice to a whisper, so that his parents wouldn't overhear. 'Or if the Grey Horse is behind this, he could be *anywhere*.'

'I'll try the cliffs first,' said Tamzin. 'From up there I can see for miles.'

'That makes sense. Oh, if only I could get out, too – I hate just sitting here doing nothing! Phone me straight away if you see any sign of him, won't you?'

'Of course! And you do the same.'

'Sure. Good luck!'

Tamzin bolted her breakfast, explaining to Nan between bites of toast and gulps of coffee. Nan was unhappy about the idea of her going off alone.

'Moonlight could be *anywhere*,' she said. 'I'm not saying you definitely won't find him, but honestly, I think the chances are very small.'

'Do *you* think the Grey Horse has taken him, Nan?' Tamzin asked.

'I don't know, pet,' Nan replied seriously. 'That's why I'm so worried. If it *is* involved in some way, then searching for Moonlight could lead you into all kinds of danger. I really don't think you should go.'

'Please, Nan, don't say I can't!' Tamzin

begged. 'Moonlight might be trapped somewhere, maybe hurt! I've *got* to look for him!'

Nan argued, but nothing would sway Tamzin, and at last she gave in. 'But you're to take your mobile, and ring me every half hour,' she said. 'If I don't hear from you, I'll be coming out myself to search for you.'

'I will, Nan.' Tamzin stood on tiptoe to kiss her cheek. 'Thank you!'

Within a few minutes she was slipping and slithering down to the path, from where she turned along the valley. The sun was trying to break through the clouds as she reached the cliff track and started to climb. The going was easier here than in the valley, for the path was stony and the torrential rain had simply streamed away. All the same, she was out of breath by the time she reached the clifftop and stopped to gaze around at the landscape.

Where was Moonlight? He had not wanted to leave the stables and go to the barn yesterday; he had tried to stop her from taking him away. Tamzin scanned the great empty vista, and an awful feeling of doubt crept into her mind. If Moonlight was free and safe he would have come to her, she felt sure of that. Something was very, very wrong – and she believed that Moonlight was in danger.

She continued to gaze around, searching for the slightest sign, the smallest clue, *anything* that might help. But all she saw was the grey-green sweep of the clifftop, patched here and there with the bright yellow of flowering gorse.

'Moonlight!' Her voice rang out across the emptiness. The only answer was the mournful cry of a gull sailing on the wind beyond the cliff edge. Could she reach him another way? Tamzin tried to focus her mind, thinking about the pony with all her willpower, trying to make contact. But, as she had feared, there was nothing.

She walked the cliffs for three hours. Every half hour she rang Nan as she had promised, but each time she had only failure to report. At last, weary and dispirited, she gave up and returned to Chapel Cottage.

'I'm so sorry, love,' Nan said sadly. 'But don't give up hope. As soon as the flood water goes down, everyone will start looking for Moonlight. We *will* find him, however long it takes.'

Tamzin only wished she could believe that. But she didn't voice her doubts to Nan. She just nodded miserably and went up to her room.

For two more days there was no news. Mr and Mrs Richards had contacted the police, but though they were sympathetic they were too busy dealing with the results of the flooding to worry much about a missing pony. The farmer was so upset that he stayed in the barn himself each night, in case the thieves should come back. They didn't, of course, and

Tamzin and Joel knew why. There *were* no thieves – at least, not the kind that anyone else would believe in.

Tamzin continued to search. But she knew in her heart it would do no good, and she was right. On the second night, she went to bed feeling more miserable than she could ever remember. It didn't matter to her that the sun had shone brilliantly all day and the wind was warm and gentle – if anything, it made matters even worse. If was as if the Grey Horse had got what it wanted, and the lovely weather was its way of mocking her.

Though she was desperately tired, she knew she would not be able to sleep, so she sat by her window in the darkness, gazing out at the moonlit garden. Near midnight she heard Nan tiptoe past on her way to bed, then the landing light went off and the house was silent.

Moonlight, oh, Moonlight, where are you? Tamzin sent the thought out into the night. Tears were trickling down her face. She wiped them away, blinking – then her hand froze in mid-air.

Far away, so far that it was hardly audible, a horse was whinnying.

Tamzin scrambled to her feet, flung the window open and leaned out. Had she imagined it? She listened hard, but the only sound was the gentle rustling of bushes in the garden.

'*Moonlight?*' She whispered the pony's name, afraid of waking Nan. For a moment there was nothing. Then, faintly, she heard the whinny a second time.

Tamzin's heart gave a huge lurch and hope surged dizzyingly. She was out of the room in seconds and scurrying along the landing. *Quietly, quietly, don't wake Nan!* She nearly fell down the stairs in her haste, and raced through to the kitchen. Baggins looked up in surprise from his favourite chair and mewed a question, but she ignored him, unbolted the back door and ran outside.

* * *

'*Moonlight!*' Her voice was still a whisper, but she mentally projected it with all her strength. '*Moonlight, I'm here!*'

The moon was behind a small cloud, but as Tamzin waited breathlessly for an answer, light appeared at the cloud's edge and it sailed into view again. The darkness was suddenly shot through with silver – and there, looking over the garden gate, was the dapple-grey pony.

'Moonlight!' Tamzin ran towards him, arms held out to hug him. Moonlight tossed his head in the way she knew so well –

Then suddenly he wasn't there any more.

Tamzin skidded to a stop, and stared in dismay at the gate. Moonlight *had* been there! She hadn't dreamed it or imagined it; she had *seen* him!

'M-Moonlight . . .?' Her voice quavered. Where had he *gone*?

Behind her she heard a soft whicker. She spun round. Moonlight had appeared again.

He was standing between her and the house, and his head was lowered as though he was very tired. Swallowing back a lurch of fear, Tamzin started towards him, more slowly this time. He didn't move, only gazed at her, and she really thought she would reach him and touch him. She stretched out a hand . . .

Moonlight vanished.

Tamzin put a clenched fist to her mouth as the fear started to turn into terror. What was happening? Was she dreaming? Or was this another vision, like the one she had had on the beach?

Then something pale flickered at the edge of her vision, and quickly she turned again. A shape was moving beyond the garden, heading down towards the valley. A horse, cantering . . . the night seemed to brighten, and she saw Moonlight clearly. He turned his head and looked back at her. Then he swung away, and his shape faded to nothing as the dark came back.

* * *

Tamzin stood motionless, alone in the garden. An awful intuition had taken hold of her, and she began to tremble as she stared into the empty night. *No*, she told herself. *No, not that . . .* But she couldn't escape from the feeling that she knew the terrible truth.

Suddenly she couldn't bear it any more, and she turned and ran back into the kitchen. Baggins mewed again but again she took no notice. She stumbled up to her room and flung herself down on the bed, burying her face in the pillows. She was so frightened and unhappy that she couldn't even cry. All she could do was lie shaking and shivering, and trying to fight the huge, suffocating pain in her mind.

Eventually she was able to crawl under the duvet again. But she did not sleep. She lay staring at her alarm clock, willing time to move faster and morning to come so that she could talk to Joel. At long last the clock's hands crept round to seven, and with the early daylight shining in at her window, she picked up her mobile and called Joel's number.

'Hi, Tam – you're up early!' Joel sounded cheerful 'Good news – the flood water's gone down enough for us to get out. So I thought –'

Tamzin said in a small, tight voice, 'Joel . . .'

'Tam? What's the matter?'

'Moonlight . . .' she whispered. 'He – came back last night.'

'*What?* That's brilliant! Where is he? Did you catch him? Is he at your place?'

'No,' said Tamzin. 'That's not what I mean. I saw him, in the garden, but . . . he wasn't really there. He looked like a . . .' Tamzin choked on the word but forced herself to say it. 'Like a *ghost*, Joel. And I had this feeling, this terrible feeling that . . . that Moonlight's *dead*.'

chapter ten

'Listen to me, Tam.' Joel gripped Tamzin's hands hard. 'You can't possibly know for sure about Moonlight! It could have been a kind of waking dream – or a vision, like the one you had on the beach. You've *got* to make yourself believe that!'

Joel had arrived at Chapel Cottage a few minutes earlier, and he and Tamzin were sitting together at the kitchen table. Nan was in her studio; tactfully, she had left them alone to talk. There was a tremendous amount of mess to be cleared at the Richardses', but Joel had been given permission to come straight away to see Tamzin. He had told his parents that it was urgent, but he had not told them any details. He only wished he could have done; for they too were anxious and upset about Moonlight. But this was too strange. They wouldn't have understood.

Tamzin nodded, biting her lip. 'I know,' she said. 'I keep telling myself I'm being stupid, and there's no reason for me to think anything's happened to Moonlight. But I've got this terrible feeling, and I can't make it go away!'

'Look,' said Joel, 'maybe the Blue Horse was trying to reach you, and it – I don't know; it put an image of Moonlight into your mind, because you trust him. Isn't that just as likely as – well, what you're thinking?'

'I suppose so . . . But what was it trying to tell me? *Something*'s going on, I know it is.'

'Well, we'd better start trying to work it out, then, hadn't we?' said Joel. 'Now that the rain's stopped and we can start getting around again, we can –'

He was interrupted by the sound of a car horn beeping outside. Tamzin got up and went to the window.

'Oh!' she said. 'It's Alec – it's been days since we heard from him.' Her face lit up eagerly. 'He might have some news about Moonlight!'

Alec Brewer saw her at the window and waved. Tamzin ran to the door to meet him.

'Alec! Is it Moonlight? Have you heard something?'

'Moonlight?' Alec was nonplussed. 'No. Why, what's happened to him?'

Tamzin's eagerness collapsed into disappointment, and Joel said, 'Tam, there's no reason why Alec should know.' He told Alec about Moonlight's disappearance.

'That's terrible!' Alec said. 'Was he stolen?'

Tamzin was about to say, 'No!' but Joel gave her a warning look.

127

* * *

'We don't know,' he said. 'It's possible, but we can't be sure.'

'Well, I'm very sorry indeed to hear it.' Alec glanced at Tamzin. 'I know he's a very special pony to you. And I understand why.'

'When you arrived just now,' said Tamzin, 'I thought – well, I just wondered if the reason why you were here was because you had some news of him.'

'I only wish I had. Though I have got news of another kind. It's the reason why I came along in person, rather than phoning.' Alec put a folder of papers down on the table. 'I've been able to translate some of the writing we found in the cave tunnel.'

Despite her preoccupation with Moonlight, Tamzin felt a sharp jab of excitement. What had Joel said only a minute ago? That maybe the Blue Horse was trying to reach her . . . And the phantom Moonlight had gone away from her in the direction of the beach . . .

'What have you found?' she asked.

'Is your nan in? I'd like her to see it, too.'

'She's in her studio. I'll get her!'

Nan came hurrying when she heard, and Alec spread the papers out on the table.

'These are the old Cornish words that were carved on the tunnel wall,' he said, pointing to the first sheet. 'We couldn't make out much, if you remember, but with the help of the library people I've been able to guess what at least some of them mean. The Cornish words are a kind of rhyme, though of course in English they sound totally different.'

'A rhyme?' Nan mused. 'That's interesting. People don't usually make rhymes unless it's something very significant.'

'Exactly what I thought,' said Alec. 'Some of the words had the library assistants foxed, but this is what they did manage to piece together.' He picked up a second sheet of paper with scribbled handwriting on it. 'It says: "Call me from this place" – then there's something they couldn't translate – "and break the power of . . ." – but the next few words were some of the ones we couldn't make out in the tunnel, so we don't know what "power" it means. Then it goes on: "With faith and courage, *something*" – again, we don't know what – "will win the day."'

Nan and Tamzin looked at each other, and Tamzin's stomach gave a little lurch. 'Break the power, and win the day,' Tamzin whispered. 'But which power, Nan? Power for good – or for evil?'

'I think the answer is in the words,' said Nan. 'The rhyme speaks of "faith and courage". The Grey Horse knows nothing about those. No; whoever carved those words was a friend to the Blue Horse. "Call me from this place" – does it mean the beach? Or the cave itself? And how to "call" . . .?' She turned quickly to Alec. 'Were you able to translate any more?'

'Not much, I'm afraid,' said Alec. 'There was one word which they thought means

* * *

"lake", but they weren't sure. I think they must be wrong. There aren't any lakes round here, are there?'

'Maybe it means a rock pool,' Joel suggested.

'Yes!' Tamzin chimed in, excited. 'The one in the cave, that we had to wade through to reach the tunnel!'

'I wouldn't think so,' said Alec, shaking his head. 'Pools like that only exist because the sea scoops the sand out; they change all the time.' He pored over the papers again. 'There are some lines here – part of what's carved in the tunnel – that completely baffled everyone who looked at them. I made a copy – here, look – but it's impossible to make out what most of the letters are.'

'It doesn't even look like an ordinary alphabet,' said Joel, peering. 'I mean, that *could* be an 'A', and maybe those are 'T's . . . but the rest don't make any sense at all, that I can see.'

'They don't, do they?' Alec agreed. 'But the letters – if they are letters – were larger than all the others, which suggests that they were particularly important to whoever carved them. If only we knew what it meant, it might tell us a lot more.'

Tamzin looked at the jumble of marks and lines . . . and at the back of her mind a peculiar feeling stirred. *Call me from this place* . . . a shiver assailed her, like a tiny current of electricity over her skin. She had the weirdest sensation that something was calling to her, urgently. She shut her eyes, trying to reach it, trying to hear what it was saying –

'Tam?' came Joel's voice. 'What's up?'

Tamzin snapped back to earth with a jolt and her eyes opened. 'I . . .' She swallowed. 'I want . . .'

'What is it, love?' Nan asked anxiously. They were all crowding round her, puzzled and concerned. And suddenly Tamzin *knew* what she had to do.

* * *

'I've got to go to the beach!' she said. 'I've got to go back to the tunnel – now, right *now*!'

Alec looked confused, but Joel looked sharply at Tamzin. He didn't know exactly what she was thinking, but her expression told him that she had sensed something. Nan, too, was staring at Tamzin's face, and her eyes had narrowed.

Joel said quickly, 'What time's low tide?'

Nan checked the kitchen clock. 'In about two hours.'

'So it'll be out past the headland by now.'

'Yes . . .'

'Nan, I've *got* to go!' Tamzin pleaded.

For a moment Nan hesitated. Then: 'All right,' she said tensely. 'But not alone, Tamzin. Joel and Alec will go with you.'

'Of course,' Alec agreed. 'But I don't understand what's so –'

Nan interrupted. 'I know you don't, Alec, but I'm just asking you to trust me.' She glanced at Joel. 'To trust all of us.'

Tamzin scrambled to her feet and started towards the porch to get her boots and coat. Then she paused. 'Will you come, too, Nan?'

'No, love. It . . . wouldn't be right. You're the guardian now; this is something you must do for yourself.' Her look stopped Alec before he could ask any more questions, and she added to him, 'Look after her. That's all I ask.'

Though Alec did not understand, the atmosphere in the room told him that this was something to be taken very seriously. He nodded, his face grave.

'I will. I promise it.'

chapter eleven

The valley path was still like a morass, so Alec drove them to the beach. As his car swung into the car park, Tamzin was surprised by what she saw. Maybe it was because of her own tension, but she had expected huge breakers to be rolling in and pounding the shore. Instead, though, the sea looked calm and almost gentle. The tide was just beyond the headland, and the sand near the water's edge shone wetly.

There were no other vehicles in the car park, and no sign of anyone on the beach.

'A lot of holidaymakers have gone home

because of the weather,' Joel said. 'Even before the worst rain started, we had loads of cancellations at the stables.'

Tamzin was already out of the car, and she fidgeted restlessly, staring towards the sea. 'Come on!' she said impatiently. 'Don't waste *time*!'

'OK, OK!' Joel was helping Alec with his pack of flashlights and ropes. 'The tide's still on its way out, and the cave isn't going anywhere!'

For a moment he thought she was going to shout back angrily. But abruptly her shoulders slumped and she sighed.

'Sorry. I've just got a feeling that we need to hurry. I don't know why.'

'Well, we're ready now,' said Alec, locking the car and pocketing the keys. 'Come on, team – onwards and upwards!'

Normally Tamzin would have laughed, or at least smiled, at his cheerfulness. This time, though, she only swung round and headed almost at a run for the rock slope that led to the sand.

Tamzin had half feared that it would no longer be possible to get into the cave. The sea might have shifted the boulders again, or there might have been another cliff fall. Instead, though, sand washed in by the tides had built up against the piled boulders, and if anything the entrance was easier to reach than it had been before.

Almost *too* easy, in fact. Tamzin looked back at the clear blue sky stretching to the horizon all the way down the coast. She didn't trust this. Everything was going so smoothly, even to the calm sea and lovely weather. She wanted to believe it was because the Blue Horse was helping her. But what if she was wrong?

Pushing the thought away, she followed Joel and Alec, who were scrambling up to the dark gap of the cave mouth. The stream was still running from the cave, still following its unnaturally straight course to the sea, like an arrow pointing towards Lion Rock. Tamzin looked at the rock, feeling as if her stomach was full of tiny wheels, spinning and whirling. She remembered her vision, thought of Moonlight . . . Alec had reached the gap and eased through, with Joel behind him. For a moment Tamzin hesitated. Then, pushing down a surge of queasy fear, she followed them into the cave.

This time they all had torches, and the combined light made the cave seem almost bright. Sand had partly filled the pool at the back, so that it was now only a few centimetres deep. The stream, Tamzin saw, emerged from a crack in the rock and flowed through the pool before spreading over the sand.

Joel had never seen the tunnel before, and

* * *

as they approached the entrance he whistled softly.

'That's amazing! Was it really the earth tremor that opened this up?'

'Can't have been anything else,' said Alec. 'And look at the shape of the hole; it's almost square. That proves it's man-made.'

They advanced into the tunnel, and Alec led the way to where the first of the carved words showed faintly on the wall. 'Here's the beginning of Tamzin's rhyme, you see,' He pointed. '"*Gweetho An Men Ma*." And these other words are the bit about calling something, and faith and courage.' He moved on a few metres. 'But *these* are the mystery marks.'

Joel shone his torch on them and stared hard, then shook his head. 'They don't mean a thing to me. Tam?'

Tamzin did not answer. She too was staring at the markings. And in her mind, too far away yet for her to grasp, a thought was forming . . .

'Where does the tunnel lead to?' Joel asked Alec.

'It could join up with an old mineshaft, or it might go right to the top of the cliff and come out there,' Alec replied. 'But I don't know yet. I was so excited when I found these carvings, I didn't go much further.'

'But what if there are more carvings, deeper in?' said Joel. 'There might even be something that'll explain these.'

Alec looked at him in surprise, then slapped a hand against his own forehead. 'What an idiot I am! I didn't even *think* of that – Joel, you could just have given us the answer we've been looking for!' In the torchlight his eyes gleamed eagerly. 'I'm going to go and look. Will you two be all right on your own for a bit?'

'Sure.' Joel glanced at Tamzin but she didn't seem to be listening.

'I won't go out of earshot,' Alec added. 'And I'll only be a few minutes.'

He strode on deeper into the tunnel. His bobbing torch beam vanished, then his footsteps faded into silence. The sea was so quiet today that Joel couldn't even hear the sound of it echoing in the cave below them. Tamzin couldn't hear it, either. She hadn't heard what Joel and Alec had said to each other, and she wasn't aware that Alec had gone. She was standing motionless in front of the wall, and with one hand she was tracing the outlines of the marks that no one had been able to decipher. Then suddenly, in a small, quavering voice, she said, 'Joel . . . I think something's trying to tell me what it says.'

'What?' Joel's eyes widened.

'It's as if there's a voice in my head, saying the words aloud,' Tamzin whispered. 'Only I can't hear properly – it's all muffled; you know, like when you're trying to remember something, and you can't . . .' She swallowed.

* * *

'There's a – a sort of pattern to it, though . . .'

'Another rhyme?'

'It could be. But . . .' Tamzin shut her eyes, biting her lip so hard that it hurt. 'I can't hear it!' she said in distress. 'It won't come! Oh, if only –'

Though she didn't know why, she had been about to say, *If only Moonlight was here*, and at the same moment she saw a picture of her lost white pony in her mind's eye. Moonlight, standing in the garden in the dark of the night, then vanishing just as she reached out to him. Tears started to stream down Tamzin's cheeks; she opened her eyes, struggling to blink them away . . .

And through blurred vision she saw that the marks on the tunnel wall were no longer the same.

'Joel!' She grabbed at his arm. 'Look – the writing!'

'What about it?'

'It's changed! Can't you see?' Then she

realized that he couldn't. This was happening
for her, and her alone. *Words* – she didn't
understand them but –

'*Margh Glas – Margh a Hav –*' She heard
her own voice speaking, saw the astonishment
on Joel's face. '*My a wra delwel – dhiworth
mor, tewes, ha men –*' Her mind lurched; the
tunnel walls seemed to rush at her and then
pull back. And in her mind, in her memory,
she heard a horse's shrill whinny.

A tingle went through her arm, and blue
light flared from the bracelet at her wrist.
When it faded, the words carved on the wall
had changed again. And now, she understood
what they were.

'Joel, it's a spell! A summoning spell, to call
the Blue Horse!' Shaking like a leaf, Tamzin
started to recite:

'Blue Horse, Horse of Summer – I call you
from sea and sand and stone –'

She got no further, for from outside came
a bellowing roar like thunder. It drowned her

voice and filled the tunnel with a deafening reverberation. Joel clapped his hands over his ears as the noise rumbled on, then as it finally faded there was the sound of running feet, and Alec appeared.

'What on earth was *that*?' In the torchlight they saw that his face was pale.

Wide-eyed, Tamzin looked from him to Joel. 'The Grey Horse . . . We've got to go! Oh, *quickly*!'

The others did not need telling twice. They started to run, heading for the safety of the outside world. They reached the tunnel mouth, slithered down the rock slope and splashed through the pool – then Tamzin stopped.

'Listen!' she said, aghast.

They could all hear it. Another roaring sound; not like thunder this time but steadier. It was all too familiar.

'The sea . . .' Joel said. 'But it was calm when we came in! How can –'

Tamzin interrupted him. 'Come on! *Hurry!*'

* * *

She was ahead when they reached the gap in the fallen boulders, but Alec called her back and went through first. Tamzin and Joel scrambled after him, and almost knocked him over as they emerged. Alec was standing on the rocks, rigid with shock.

'Good heavens,' he said in an awed voice, 'Where did *that* come from?'

In the space of a few minutes the calm sea had turned into a chaos of pounding, heaving surf. Enormous breakers crashed and clashed together, hurling spray high into the air. And where before there had been clear blue sky, a vast cloud the colour of a dark and angry bruise was spreading towards the coast from far out to sea, driven on a wild wind.

Tamzin's hair streamed out behind her as she stared at the scene, and the terrifying truth came to her. She knew, now, that the words on the tunnel wall would summon the Blue Horse, and she had started to say them aloud. But the Grey Horse had heard – and in its fury it would do anything to stop the spell from being spoken!

Suddenly the rock under her feet seemed to move, almost throwing her off balance. Joel reached out to steady her, and they all jumped down on to the sand. But the sand was moving, too; vibrating, shaking –

'Oh no,' said Alec, 'it's another tremor! Get off the beach – *run*!'

He grabbed one each of their hands, and they pelted away from the cave. As if the sea was adding its own warning, a fresh roar dinned in their ears as a colossal wave broke behind them. The ground juddered again; Joel tripped and would have fallen, but Alec heaved him back on to his feet and they raced on. Round the headland – Tamzin's legs felt as if they were on fire, and her boots were dragging weights on her feet. But she ploughed on, stumbling and jumping over the quaking sand.

Then, just as they reached the slope to the

* * *

car park, the tremor stopped. It was so sudden that Tamzin lost her footing and went sprawling. She started to pick herself up – and froze as she saw the sky.

The cloud was spreading fast, almost covering the blue completely now. As it spread, it was changing. A shape was rising from its towering top, curling over, taking on clear form. And with stark horror Tamzin recognized the huge, menacing head of a grey horse.

What have I done? The thought slammed through her head and she stared numbly at the cloud, trying desperately not to believe it. Then Joel's voice broke the thrall.

'The spell, Tam! Say it! *Say it!*'

He shook her, almost screaming in his effort to bring her back to earth. Tamzin's mind reeled as she struggled to remember the words on the cave wall. She had *seen* them, she *knew* them – but she could no longer recall them.

* * *

'It's gone!' she wailed. 'Oh, Joel, I can't remember it!'

'Think!' Joel yelled. 'You started to say it in the tunnel – something about summer – and sand and sea and stone –'

Sand, sea, stone – the trigger worked, and words flooded into Tamzin's mind. She scrabbled to her feet, turning to face the gusting wind, and her voice rang out above the tide's roar.

'Blue Horse, Horse of Summer! I call you from sea and sand and stone! Blue Horse, come to us! Blue Horse, help us in our danger!' She flung out one arm, the arm that wore the bracelet. '*Margh Glas, difun!* Blue Horse, *awake*!'

A jolt like an electric shock went up her arm as light flared from the glass talisman. She heard Alec cry out in surprise – then with no warning, the ground began to shake again, far more violently than before. Suddenly it humped and lifted, as though a buried giant had hunched his shoulders. They were all thrown off their feet and fell heavily to the sand. Gasping, Tamzin tried to sit up, but the ground still quivered. Stones were rolling down the slope, and from the cliffs came an ominous rumble. Then suddenly Joel shouted, 'Look, Tam! Oh, *look*!'

He was pointing at the car park and the valley beyond. Tamzin turned dizzily around.

Along the valley path, something was racing towards them. It was moving at astonishing speed, flowing and flickering as it came. Something streamed behind it, looking like pale smoke. But it was not smoke. It was the flying mane and tail of a dappled white horse.

Tamzin's heart seemed to swell inside her and she screamed, '*Moonlight!*'

chapter twelve

They could all see Moonlight clearly now –
but he was not the Moonlight they had
known. No earthly horse could have moved at
such a speed; his hooves seemed to fly, barely
touching the ground as he galloped towards
them. And as he drew nearer, the colour of
his coat was changing from white to blue.

Alec was still on his hands and knees,
staring in sheer disbelief. Tamzin and Joel
clung to each other. They couldn't speak;
couldn't explain to him. They could only
watch with a thrill of excitement as the racing
vision reached the car park and rushed on

towards the slope. As he reached the edge a howl erupted from the sky; Moonlight tossed his head and answered with a shrill scream. Then he took off in an astounding leap that carried him over the boulders to the sand. Blue light blazing around him, he streaked past the three and away towards the sea. The tide rushed to meet him; as he plunged into the breakers his mane and tail mingled with the spray. Then he became one with the crashing breakers and was gone. Tamzin heard herself cry out – and as she did so, a new wave began to rise. It towered high, sapphire blue against the threatening cloud. Then it surged away from the shore to the deep sea.

The grey head of the cloud curled and twisted and seemed to rear up in fury. The blue wave was heading for Lion Rock – and suddenly a part of the cloud began to whirl. It formed into a cone, and the cone started to spin downwards, stretching towards the wave, reaching for it as though to stab it like a huge dagger.

The wave rose to meet it. They touched, and in an explosion of grey and blue the two became a swaying, whirling column, joining the sky with the sea.

'It's a waterspout!' Alec yelled above the noise of the elements.

Still clasping each other, Tamzin and Joel watched the incredible turmoil as the two huge forces clashed. The spinning column was moving closer and closer to Lion Rock, and despite the wind blowing in her face Tamzin felt as if there was no air left in the world to breathe. This was no mere waterspout – it was a battle between two ancient enemies. And if the Grey Horse should triumph, the future was too terrible to think of.

But it seemed that the Grey Horse *would* triumph. To her horror, she saw that the stuff of the cloud was spiralling faster, forcing down the spinning tower of water. The column was almost completely grey now, and the Blue Horse was falling back, its power weakening. She had to do something! But what *could* she do? She was helpless –

YOU ARE NOT HELPLESS! The words rose in her mind and filled her head, so unexpectedly that she gasped and staggered backwards. *THE SPELL, TAMZIN! THE TALISMAN, AND THE SPELL – SAY IT AGAIN! SAY IT NOW!*

Almost without her willing it, Tamzin's arm stretched upwards, the glass charm glittering on her wrist. 'Blue Horse!' Her voice was shrill above the roar of sea and wind. 'Horse of Summer! I call you from sea and sand and stone!'

As the words of the ancient summoning rang out, the base of the waterspout shuddered violently. The colour of the column began to change – and as Tamzin screamed, '*Blue Horse, awake!*' the battling forces struck Lion Rock. The sea seemed to erupt as new energy flowed upwards. The entire waterspout turned brilliant blue, and with a noise like echoing thunder it surged up into the cloud. The grey shape in the sky was torn apart, and as it collapsed, a wave began to rise –

'Move!' Alec yelled at the top of his voice. 'Get to the car park!'

All three of them fled, leaping over the boulders and up the slope as the wave rushed shorewards. They heard the crash as it broke, but there was no time to look back until they gained high ground and slid to a breathless stop.

The wave came piling and foaming up the beach and over the sand where they had been standing less than a minute ago. Spray burst over the rocks and blotted out the view, but the power of the torrent was spent. The spray cleared; the water began to fall back.

And the great grey cloud was gone. Tamzin, Joel and Alec stood staring at a calm sea, blue as sapphires under the bright spring sun.

* * *

For a minute or more no one moved, and no one spoke. Then, in a low, unsteady voice, Joel said,

'Look at the rock . . .'

The familiar shape of Lion Rock had changed. Where before there had been a single crag, now there were two; as though a tremendous force had sheared through the Rock and split it.

A tremendous force . . . Tamzin started to shiver and could not make herself stop. The Blue Horse had won the battle. But what had become of Moonlight? Tears started to her eyes; she raised a hand to wipe them away, not wanting Joel and Alec to see. Then she stopped as, through blurred vision, she saw something glinting among the rocks below her.

With a lurch of intuition she scrambled down the rocks to where the glinting thing lay. The great wave must have washed it in; she bent down to pick it up . . .

A third fragment of glass shimmered
between her fingers. It was blue like the others,
but there was a hint of green in it, like the
green of the winter sea. Slowly, holding her
breath, Tamzin touched it to the talisman on
her bracelet. Blue-green light flared as the old
and new glass fragments glowed brilliantly . . .
then the glow faded, and the new piece had
fused with the others.

And just for a moment, in the depths of the
glass, she saw a tiny image reflected. The
image of a galloping white pony.

Tamzin understood. She turned to Joel, the
tears streaming now, and whispered, 'He's
gone.'

Joel held her hands. Behind him, Alec was
rubbing at his own eyes, as if he was waking
up from a dream – or thought he was.

'Come on, Tam,' said Joel. 'Let's go home.'

Tamzin stood at her bedroom window,
watching Alec's car drive away. Joel was in the

passenger seat; he would phone later, but for now Tamzin was glad to be alone.

Alec had hardly said a word since they returned to Chapel Cottage. Tamzin wondered what he was thinking now. Perhaps he would never really believe what had happened, but would remember it as a kind of hallucination, like a waking dream. And perhaps that was just as well.

She held her glass talisman up to the window, watching the light reflect from it in tiny, winking pinpoints, and she thought of Moonlight. She would never see him again; not in any ordinary way. But in that moment on the beach, she had known the truth about him. He had never been a mortal pony at all. He *was* the Blue Horse; and through these past months he had been gaining in strength, helped – she believed – by her own efforts to combat the dark power of his ancient enemy. That growing strength had been enough for him to spirit himself away from the barn on

the night of the rainstorm: he had known
what the Grey Horse was planning, and he
had needed to be near her, to try to show
her what she must do. And she had done it.
For the spell with which she had summoned
him had enabled him to become his real self
at last.

She turned to where Nan's painting of the
galloping horse hung in its place on the wall,
and reached out to stroke the painted face. It
felt warm, almost real, and she said sadly,
'Oh, Moonlight . . . I'm going to miss you
so much.'

Yet as she spoke the words, she knew deep
down that this was not the end of it. The Grey
Horse had been defeated once more, but its
dark spirit was still free. It was out there
somewhere. Plotting. Waiting.

'I know this isn't over yet, Moonlight,'
Tamzin said to the picture. 'But whatever
the Grey Horse tries to do, you'll be with me.
I know you will. And I'm not afraid.'

Nothing wonderful happened. The sea in the painting did not begin to move, and the galloping horse did not come to life. But Tamzin believed that the Blue Horse had heard her.

And when the time came for the final test, he would return.

SeaHorses

Book 1

Ride into mystery and adventure in the first exciting Sea Horses *fantasy*

According to legend, centuries ago a cruel spirit horse from the sea was trapped in a tiny statue. If it is ever set free, then wild storms, treacherous tides and terrible destruction will follow. But Tamzin is fascinated by the statue and slowly, irresistibly, she is drawn under its dark spell . . .

SeaHorses

The Talisman

Ride into more mysterious adventures in the second intriguing Sea Horses *fantasy*

The tiny statue of the Grey Horse has been broken and the cruel spirit horse is free to bring havoc and terror once again. Tamzin is afraid, especially after losing the blue talisman she wears to ward off evil. As the power of the Grey Horse takes hold, Tamzin is drawn deeper and deeper into danger . . .

SeaHorses

Book 4

The adventure draws to its exciting conclusion

Tamzin is trying to come to terms with the loss of Moonlight, but feels sure that he is still trying to protect her from the Grey Horse and keeping the evil force at bay. But how long can it last? Tamzin can't help thinking that the Grey Horse still has some unpleasant surprises in store . . .

hotnews@puffin

Hot off the press!

You'll find all the latest exclusive Puffin news here

Where's it happening?

Check out our author tours and events programme

Bestsellers

What's hot and what's not? Find out in our charts

E-mail updates

Sign up to receive all the latest news
straight to your e-mail box

Links to the coolest sites

Get connected to all the best author web sites

Book of the Month

Check out our recommended reads

www.puffin.co.uk

Read more in Puffin

For complete information about books available from Puffin – and Penguin – and how to order them, contact us at the appropriate address below. Please note that for copyright reasons the selection of books varies from country to country.

www.puffin.co.uk

In the United Kingdom: Please write to Dept EP, Penguin Books Ltd, Bath Road, Harmondsworth, West Drayton, Middlesex UB7 ODA

In the United States: Please write to Penguin Group (USA), Inc., P.O. Box 12289, Dept B, Newark, New Jersey 07101–5289 or call 1–800–788–6262

In Canada: Please write to Penguin Books Canada Ltd, 10 Alcorn Avenue, Suite 300, Toronto, Ontario M4V 3B2

In Australia: Please write to Penguin Books Australia Ltd, 250 Camberwell Road, Camberwell, Victoria 3124

In New Zealand: Please write to Penguin Group (NZ), Private Bag 102902, North Shore Mail Centre, Auckland 10

In India: Please write to Penguin Books India Pvt Ltd, 11 Panscheel Shopping Centre, Panscheel Park, New Delhi 110 017

In the Netherlands: Please write to Penguin Books Netherlands bv, Postbus 3507, NL–1001 AH Amsterdam

In Germany: Please write to Penguin Books Deutschland GmbH, Metzlerstrasse 26, 60594 Frankfurt am Main

In Spain: Please write to Penguin Books S. A., Bravo Murillo 19, 1° B, 28015 Madrid

In Italy: Please write to Penguin Italia s.r.l., Via Felice Casati 20, I–20124 Milano

In France: Please write to Penguin France S. A., 17 rue Lejeune, F–31000 Toulouse

In Japan: Please write to Penguin Books Japan, Ishikiribashi Building, 2–5–4, Suido, Bunkyo-ku, Tokyo 112

In South Africa: Please write to Longman Penguin Southern Africa (Pty) Ltd, Private Bag X08, Bertsham 2013